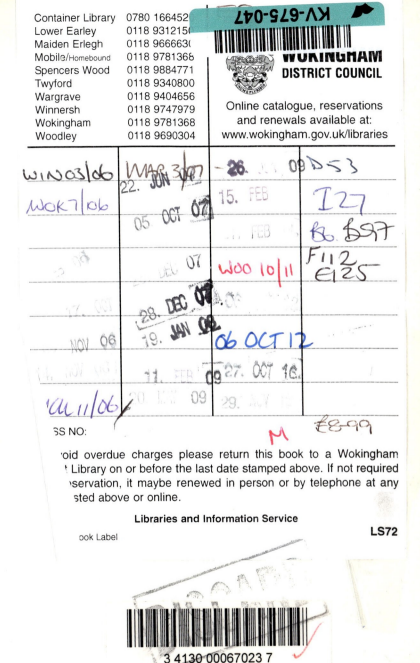

MURDER IN DUPLICATE

When Jennifer Prentice, a student nurse, was found dead in a locked bathroom, Inspector Newton went to St. Aldhelm's Hospital to investigate ... Newton finds the Matron, Miss Diana Digby Scott, unapproachable. Why was Alison Carter so disliked by Jennifer? Is Vernon Pritchard, the surgeon who was having an affair with Jennifer, telling the truth? Before Newton finds any answers, there is another death and he faces mortal danger himself.

PETER CONWAY

MURDER IN DUPLICATE

Complete and Unabridged

LINFORD
Leicester

First published in Great Britain by
Robert Hale Limited
London

First Linford Edition
published 2006
by arrangement with
Robert Hale Limited
London

British Library CIP Data

Conway, Peter
    Murder in duplicate.—Large print ed.—
Linford mystery library
    1. Detective and mystery stories
    2. Large type books
    I. Title
    823.9'14 [F]

    ISBN 1–84617–225–X

Published by
F. A. Thorpe (Publishing)
Anstey, Leicestershire

Set by Words & Graphics Ltd.
Anstey, Leicestershire
Printed and bound in Great Britain by
T. J. International Ltd., Padstow, Cornwall

This book is printed on acid-free paper

1

Alison Carter wriggled her toes and shifted her position slightly on top of her bed, feeling her heart beginning to beat more rapidly and a slight sinking sensation in the pit of her stomach. It was always the same; whenever she approached the climax of the thriller she was reading — and this was a particularly good one — she had to force herself not to look at the end and intensified the pleasurable suspense by deliberately reading more slowly.

She was so bound up in the book that at first she failed to notice the sounds that were coming from the next room, but then the shout of laughter and what followed, made it absolutely impossible for her to concentrate. Alison banged the book down on the bedside table and covered her ears with her hands; that was no good either, she could even feel the vibration coming through the floor. What

1

made it worse was that, in addition to her feelings of disgust, she was also excited by what she could hear. Why was it so difficult to behave in the way she knew was right?

There was another high pitched cry and suddenly she could stand it no longer.

'Pigs!' she shouted at the top of her voice and hit the wall a couple of times as hard as she could with her pillow.

The noises were cut off abruptly and for a moment there was complete silence, shortly followed by a shriek of laughter and a series of violent thumps on the other side of the wall. Alison heard the window in the next room being thrown open and the shouted obscenity was followed by a doubling in the intensity of the previous sounds. She listened for a moment, then slammed her own window shut and shaking with anger, ran out of the room.

It was pleasantly cool out in the grounds of the hospital and she strode down the road towards the main gate, trying to get out of her mind what she had heard and, even worse, what she had felt. She glanced at her watch and saw that there was only half an hour to go before they were supposed to be back inside the hospital, not that that mattered with old Flowerdew on the gate. The thought of the night porter made up her mind for her; she had often paused to have a chat with him when she came in at night and now, more than anything else, she wanted to talk to someone.

Flowerdew was standing outside the lodge near the main gate with his hands behind his back, peering benignly through his rimless spectacles. He was a short, fat, fresh-complexioned man with a ruff of snow white hair, which set off the pink, bald crown of his head. When he thought about it, which was not often, he realized what a curious life he had led. He had worked at the hospital for forty-five years and for the last thirty-five of them as night porter on the gate. During that time he had never had a holiday and yet was perfectly happy with his lot. In the summer, he liked nothing better than to savour the night air, listen to the familiar noises and study the stars, while in the winter, there was always the snug warmth of the little room behind the office.

He turned as he heard the footsteps approaching and watched the girl as she hurried towards him. Flowerdew was a mine of information about train time-tables, bus routes and what was on at the local cinema and he assumed that she was going to ask him something, but as she drew close, he could see that something had upset her badly. Her face was flushed, she was breathing heavily and when she spoke, there was an obvious tremor in her voice.

'Hello, Mr Flowerdew.'

'Hello, my dear, what can I do for you?'

'I was just going for a stroll before going to bed and seeing you here, thought I'd drop in for a chat.'

'How very nice! What about a cup of tea? I was just about to put the kettle on.'

He heard her sigh and then her face broke into a smile. 'That would be lovely, it's just what I could do with.'

'Better come inside. If Miss Digby Scott saw us chatting together, I'd never hear the last of it.'

The old man chuckled. There had been times — quite a few times in fact — when he had dispensed a good bit more than cups of tea to the nurses in the little room behind the office, but that had been many years ago and he hadn't been bad looking in those days, even though he said it himself.

As he followed the girl in, he admired her trim figure; it was true that he preferred nurses in their uniforms, but he had to admit that there was something about tight jeans, particularly if their wearer was slim enough. Now that he could see her under the light, he was even more sure of his instinct that something had upset her badly and he had a shrewd suspicion what it was — he hadn't been the confidant of young doctors and nurses for all those years for nothing.

'I was just thinking as you walked by,' he said, plugging in the electric kettle and taking the tea caddy down from its shelf, 'that I have been in this particular job for thirty-five years and I've enjoyed every minute of it.'

'Don't you get fed up with being on night duty all the time?'

'Bless you no; I love it. This is home to me, you know.' He sighed. 'I'm due to retire in a couple of years time and I don't know what I'll do with myself then, I really don't.'

'We'll have to organize a public petition to allow you to stay on.'

'You might have succeeded in Miss Massey's day, but not now; too many new brooms about the place to my way of thinking.'

'I know what you mean.'

'So you sense it too, do you? This hospital isn't the happy place it used to be, you know; when you've been around as long as I have, you can feel it.' He shook his head dolefully.

'Come now, it's not as bad as all that.'

Flowerdew handed the cup of tea across and beamed at her. 'To think I asked you in here because I thought you needed cheering up, and here am I telling you all my troubles.'

'Was it all that obvious?'

'Not really, to be truthful, it was just an

excuse for an old man to talk to a pretty girl. Now I've gone and embarrassed you,' he added, seeing her blush.

'That's just my trouble — I'm always being embarrassed.'

'That's nothing to be ashamed of — it makes a nice change. Do you know, the other day, one of the lady house officers — they didn't have such things when I was first here — actually came to ask me if her knickers had been handed in; said she'd lost them in the grounds!' He raised one eyebrow quizzically.

Alison laughed. 'Had they been?'

'No, but I thought I'd have a bit of fun and said that Mr Pritchard had brought them in that morning.'

'What was her reaction to that?'

'She didn't turn a hair and cool as you please said: 'I'm not surprised. I didn't actually see who it was, but I was quite sure it was one of the consultants.' 'How was that then?' I asked. 'He made me do all the work.''

Alison choked on her tea. 'Mr Flowerdew, you're an old rogue; you'll get done for criminal libel if you're not careful.'

★ ★ ★

The couple on the bed sprang apart when they heard the loud thump on the other side of the wall. After a moment's silence, the dark haired girl leaned across, picked up the bedside lamp and pounded the wall with it, ignoring the flakes of plaster that began to chip off. She then jumped off the bed and threw the window open.

'Belt up, you moronic cow,' she shouted at the top of her voice, then began to laugh maniacally.

'For God's sake Jennifer! You've gone too far this time; Miss Digby Scott's bound to have heard that, her flat's only a couple of floors up.'

'Who cares? I can't think why someone hasn't stood up to her long ago; you seem to forget that Florence Nightingale died over sixty years ago.'

The girl went across to the window and put her head outside once more.

'Jennifer! Come back at once.'

She turned round with a twisted smile on her face. 'Make me.'

He gripped her wrist, but she bent

forward and bit him hard on the back of his hand.

'You little bitch.'

The blow caught her across the mouth and a thin trickle of blood began to descend from her lip. For a moment she stood there immobile, then she came at him, kicking, punching, biting and scratching.

★   ★   ★

Ian Moore sat back in the easy chair and drew in deeply on his cigarette, watching the girl lying naked on the bed. Even after all that had happened, she seemed incapable of keeping still, fidgeting constantly and playing with a lock of her hair.

'That's it, you know Jennifer. I'm not coming here again. Why the hell no one came down, I don't know. If I'm caught in your room I'll never get a reference.'

'With your uncle eating out of your hand, I don't see what you've got to worry about.'

'He hasn't much influence away from

here and I can't stay for ever. Another thing, too, I've received an anonymous letter.'

'That's nothing, I've had two.' She pulled open the drawer of the bedside table and took out a piece of paper. 'I threw the first one away, it was some rot about the wages of sin being death, and then this was pushed under the door soon after your last visit.' She began to read in a theatrical voice. ''You have been warned. Next time, if there is a next time, will be the last time.''

'Well, you may laugh, but I don't like it. I've a shrewd idea who it is myself, but what do you think?'

'Who else but that frustrated virgin next door — anyone can see that she's really dying for it. I'll tell you something, I've got plans for our friend Alison.' She giggled and jumped off the bed, whispering something in his ear. 'You can join in if you like.'

'Jennifer, you make me sick.'

'Come off it. I bet you're dying to get the opportunity. Have you forgotten how she turned down God's gift to woman-hood.'

Ian Moore got up and left the room. He was not averse to a bit of fun, but there were limits and Jennifer had reached them.

★   ★   ★

Jennifer Prentice woke up with a start ten minutes later. It took her a moment or two to come fully to her senses and she was just thinking that she couldn't raise the energy to wash or do her teeth, when she saw the plain brown envelope which had been pushed under the door. The sight of it was enough to jerk her into complete wakefulness and she jumped out of bed. She was at the door in a second, wrenched it open and stood listening in the corridor. There was no one in sight and only the distant sound of a Sinatra record broke the silence.

Ignoring the fact that she had nothing on, she went up to Alison Carter's door and tried the handle. It was locked and there was no light showing underneath, but she pounded on the woodwork with her fist.

'I know you're there, Alison. Just you wait — I'll get you for this.'

She went back into her room, muttering to herself and sat on the bed, ripping open the envelope, which she threw over her shoulder. She scanned the note with its now familiar patchwork of words obviously cut out of the daily paper and snorted with derision — it was just like Alison to go all literary on her.

She was far too wide awake to get back into bed and in any case, was feeling hot and sticky, so she slipped into her dressing-gown and made for the bathroom, which was situated on the same floor of the nurses' home. It contained two cubicles and in addition there was a hand basin in the space outside. The partition separating the two baths was made of hard-board and finished about nine inches short of the ceiling. The engaged sign was showing on the door of the first cubicle and she pushed open the second, operating the sliding catch without looking to see what she was doing, and turned on the taps of the bath.

When Jennifer came to hang her dressing-gown on the back of the door, she noticed that it had come open an inch or two and on inspecting it more closely, saw that the slot into which the sliding bar was supposed to fit, had been removed. Typical, she thought, the whole place is falling to pieces. There wasn't even anything with which to jam the door — the chair which was usually by the side of the bath was also missing — but that didn't worry her, it wasn't as if she cared if anyone did come in.

By the time she had been in the bath for five minutes, the warm water had begun to do its work and gradually she began to feel more relaxed. She gently touched the livid marks on the insides of her thighs, which were already beginning to turn purple; perhaps it would be wise to cool things down a bit, it wasn't as if Ian Moore was her only worry. She liked nursing and Ian had been quite right, if they had been caught, she would certainly have been thrown out; unlike him, she had no rich and influential uncle to bail her out if things went wrong.

Her leg suddenly gave a violent jerk, spilling some water on to the floor and she had a vision of the writhing travesty of a human being whom she had visited so often and whom she had more and more difficulty in getting out of her mind. Jennifer let out a cry of horror and closed her eyes, resting her head against the back of the bath. Was she being punished for all she had done in the last few years? That was surely nonsense; she didn't believe in God and anyhow, none of it had been her fault. She settled herself more comfortably and after a few minutes drifted off to sleep and did not stir when the door of the cubicle was gently eased open.

Jennifer was in the middle of a confused dream when she felt the firm grip on her ankles. Her eyes flicked open and then widened with surprise as she recognized the figure bending over her. She opened her mouth to scream, tried to grip the slippery sides of the bath and kicked out furiously with her legs. It was no good — the grip on her ankles was inexorable.

The girl's assailant pulled upwards violently and Jennifer slid along the bottom of the bath, her cry turning to a gurgling moan as the water shot up her nose and into her mouth. The stooping figure held on for several minutes, even though it was obvious that the girl had died instantly, then dropped her heels on either side of the taps and gave a grim smile of satisfaction.

★　★　★

Alison Carter felt considerably more cheerful when she left old Flowerdew, but was still furious with herself; if only she could take herself, and everything else for that matter, a little less seriously. What if Jennifer Prentice did make a fool of herself by throwing herself at every available male? Her own time would come, but only when she met someone with whom she could settle down happily and marry. But supposing she never did? Immediately she was livid with herself for

15

thinking about the subject again; perhaps she was in the wrong job. The trouble with the hospital was that all the men, and that even seemed to include old Flowerdew, had one-track minds and to be fair, so did the women as well. The only exception seemed to be Miss Digby Scott who, like Miss Buss and Miss Beale, appeared to be immune to Cupid's darts.

By the time she had got back to her room again, she felt much better and a little later, was even whistling cheerfully to herself as she went along the corridor towards the bathroom, her towel over her shoulder and twirling her sponge bag by its string. There had been no sound from Jennifer's room and there was no one about. Alison pushed the bathroom door open with her foot and saw with irritation that the engaged signs were showing on both cubicles. She pounded on the door of the first one.

'Will you be long?'

'Who is it?'

'It's me, Alison.'

'Give us a chance. I've only just got in.

Why not try next door, it was occupied when I got here and I haven't heard a sound since.'

'O.K. I know you Sarah, you'll be in there for hours.'

She thumped hard on the wood-work and then did it again when there was no response.

'I'm going to take a look over the top. Do you think someone's been taken ill in there?'

'Oh leave her alone Alison. The poor girl is probably just having a well-earned sleep.'

'She can jolly well do her sleeping in bed; I want a bath.'

Alison moved the chair from its place by the side of the basin, put it against the door, clambered up and looked over the top.

'God!'

'What's up?'

'It's Jennifer, she's under the water. Go and get help. Quick!'

Sarah's face appeared over the top of the partition. For a second she looked in horror at the white face staring up at her from under the water, then her mouth came open and she began to scream.

'Shut up!' shouted Alison at the top of her voice and the scream was abruptly cut off. 'That's not going to do her any good; pull yourself together and go and fetch someone. Get on to the switchboard and send for the cardiac resuscitation team. Hurry!'

It was a desperately tight fit and she had to take off her dressing-gown first, but somehow she managed to squeeze through the gap above the door and jump down on to the floor. She pulled the girl's head out of the water, simultaneously wrenching out the plug, and, awkward though the position was, started mouth to mouth breathing.

Alison realized as soon as she had started that it was going to be a waste of time, but she persevered and even tried cardiac massage until she heard the rumble of the trolley and the sound of running feet along the corridor.

Alison got out of the bath and was just about to shoot the catch across, when she realized that she wasn't wearing a stitch.

It was the work of a moment to slip on the dressing-gown hanging on the hook behind the door and let them in.

They put down an endo-tracheal tube, they respired her, they continued cardiac massage, they even injected a stimulant into her heart, but it was no good. Jennifer Prentice was dead.

The doctor in charge of the resuscitation team eventually straightened his aching back and as he left, squeezed Alison's arm. 'You did everything you could; no one could have saved her. Are you all right?'

'Yes thanks.'

Alison couldn't bear to stay in the room a moment longer and walked slowly back up the corridor. She couldn't get the vision of Jennifer's staring face out of her mind's eye or the memory of her first sight of the girl under the water. She was no stranger to death and it had never worried her before, but it was quite another matter when it was someone she knew, even if she didn't like her.

It was only when she plunged her hands deeply into the pockets of the dressing-gown and felt the crumpled piece of paper that she realized that it wasn't hers. Back in her bedroom she smoothed the letter out and laid it on the dressing-table under the light.

'That's odd,' she said to herself, a worried frown on her face.

It wasn't until that moment that the possibility of Jennifer's death being due to other than natural causes or a tragic accident, occurred to her. Although she felt self-conscious about it, she didn't get into bed until she had checked to see that the window was securely fastened, the door was locked and she had jammed the chair under the handle. She most certainly couldn't face the prospect of going back to the bathroom to fetch her own dressing-gown.

Alison hardly slept at all that night. Not only was she profoundly upset by what had happened to Jennifer, but she couldn't think what was the best thing to do about the anonymous note, which she couldn't even understand. She could always throw it away, but if someone had murdered Jennifer, it would clearly be irresponsible to do so. In that case, if she did decide to show it to someone, who would be the best person? Miss Digby Scott was the obvious choice, but Alison had always found her totally unapproachable and could only too easily imagine her reaction.

'An anonymous letter Nurse Carter?' There would be the characteristic sniff of disapproval and a slight tilting back of her head. 'Is this meant to be a joke? I've always tried to impress on you girls the need for a sense of duty and responsibility.'

She would then be good for a homily on the old-fashioned virtues, which had now so sadly lapsed, which would go on for at least ten minutes. No, Alison decided, she couldn't face Miss Digby Scott.

What about Miss Fordham, the Sister Tutor? There were rumours about Miss Fordham and, as judged by her own experience on one occasion, only too likely to be true. Miss Fordham was also undoubtedly out of the question.

And so, although she was tempted to

send it by post and knowing full well that she might be going on a fool's errand, she decided to take the note up to the police in London. The journey only took an hour and a half and she was able to go the following day during her time off.

When Alison arrived at the Yard, she was almightily glad that she had telephoned first to say that she was coming; it had been so much easier to make an appointment without getting involved in long explanations than it would have been if she had turned up unannounced at the reception desk.

She was only kept waiting for about ten minutes, but this was long enough for her to get thoroughly agitated and if she hadn't already given her name and address, she might well have walked out. Alison got out of her chair when a tall, dark man in his early thirties came into the room and advanced towards her with his hand outstretched.

'Miss Carter? So sorry to have kept you waiting. Do sit down. My name is Newton, Inspector Newton. Now, what can I do for you?'

Once she had started to tell him what had happened, all Alison's nervousness left her; the Inspector was a good listener and didn't interrupt at all.

'And so you see Inspector, I didn't know what to do for the best — I hope I'm not wasting your time.'

'You're certainly not doing that — you were quite right to come.'

'There was just one other thing.'

'What's that?'

'No one at the hospital need know that I have been to see you, need they?'

'Don't worry about that. The girl's death is bound to be reported to the coroner and it will be quite easy to explain the reason for any enquiries we have to make. Did you know this girl Jennifer at all well?'

'Not particularly; she was one of my set, but not a special friend of mine.'

'Have you any reason to think that anyone might have wanted to kill her?'

'Not the slightest. It was only when I discovered this piece of paper that I began to wonder and I realize that there may be some perfectly innocent explanation for it. By the way, what do you think it means?'

Newton hesitated for a moment and then decided that he didn't feel up to explaining to a twenty-year-old girl and a very pretty one at that, what 'the beast with two backs' meant.

'I'm not sure,' he said lamely. 'I think it may be a quotation. Well, I won't keep you any longer. Thank you again for reporting this. If any further enquiries are made, I will almost certainly have to question you again in much more detail, but as you found the body, the hospital authorities will accept it quite naturally, I'm sure.'

★　★　★

Roger Newton took the note along to his chief, Commander Osborne, as soon as Alison had left. The large thick-set man behind the desk listened in silence until he had finished and then looked morosely at the piece of paper.

'"You have been warned. Death will come to the beast with two backs.' All

24

right Newton, you can stop looking so smug — we haven't all had the doubtful benefits of a University education, you know. Let's have it, what does it mean?'

'Well sir, it's a quotation from Othello — by Shakespeare you know.'

'Don't try me too hard Newton,' Osborne growled ominously.

'I'm sorry sir.'

'I bet you are. Come along man, out with it.'

''Making the beast with two backs' is Iago's way of describing what Othello and Desdemona were up to in the privacy of their bed-chamber.'

'Very delicately put, I must say. Well, there's probably nothing in it — very curious sense of humour the medical profession seems to go in for — but you'd better get on to the coroner's officer down there. They'll be ordering an autopsy in any case, but in view of this letter the coroner will probably want one of the expert forensic chaps to do it and will no doubt agree to put off the inquest while you make enquiries. You'd also better get down there yourself and liaise with the local police. Death in a nurses' home is just up your street, I don't doubt, but perhaps you'd better take Wainwright with you. It won't do you any harm to have a chaperon, although if half of what I hear is true, it won't do any harm either for you to keep an eye on him as well.'

2

Newton had only met Golding, the forensic pathologist, once before. He had taken an instant dislike to him then and the passage of time had done nothing to make him modify his opinion. The man positively revelled in his job; the more sordid and unpleasant a situation was, the better he liked it.

The pathologist came stumping out of the postmortem room, still wearing his rubber apron and boots and coughed fruitily without bothering to remove the cigarette from the corner of his mouth. A shower of ash shot towards the detective, who was unable to hide his grimace of distaste.

'Ah, there you are Inspector. Be with you in a moment.'

He disappeared into the changing room, leaving his secretary standing nervously in the corridor, fingering her shorthand pad and a sheaf of forms.

Golding reappeared a few minutes later, snatched the forms from the secretary without saying a word and thrust open the door to his office with quite unnecessary force.

'Ring up the hospital and find out if there are any messages will you, then wait in the car?'

Please and thank you were clearly not in his vocabulary and Newton could only assume that the secretary was one of those women who enjoyed being trampled on; certainly Golding was only too willing and able to do the trampling.

The pathologist sat down at the desk and went through the elaborate ritual of lighting his pipe.

'Of course,' he said after a long interval, 'it's impossible to be certain of the cause of death until the results of the chemical analysis and microscopic studies are ready, but my guess is that no cause will be found.' Newton raised one eyebrow. 'Yes, this is a most interesting case. You see, although the girl was found under the water, I am quite certain that she didn't die as the result of drowning.'

The Inspector's interest was betrayed by the slight tightening of his lips. 'Really?'

'Yes. In death by drowning, there is froth at the mouth and nose, the lungs are bulky and ballooned, there are asphyxial haemorrhages, the great veins are engorged and the eyelids are swollen. The changes are in many ways similar to those of asphyxia produced by strangulation.'

' 'But see, his face is black and full of blood,
His eyeballs further out than when he lived.' '

'Precisely. The Bard had a way of putting these things. None of them, though, was present in this girl's case. No, she died either before or at the moment when she went under the water.'

'But how common is sudden death in previously fit girls of twenty?'

'Oh, it can happen all right. Subarachnoid haemorrhage, pulmonary embolism, now that so many girls of this age are on the pill — there are a number of causes, but I found no evidence of any of them. In this case, I am irresistibly reminded of George Joseph Smith.'

'The brides in the bath man?'

'Exactly.'

'But I thought his victims were drowned.'

'You're quite right about two of them, Elizabeth Mundy, the woman for whose murder he was hanged and Margaret Lofty, but not the third. I have made something of a study of the case and it is quite clear that the death of Alice Burnham was not caused by asphyxiation — very little water was found in the lungs. It is my theory, and to be fair, not only mine, that when he pulled her legs up sharply, the sudden inrush of water into the nasopharynx produced a reflex cardiac inhibition. To put it simply, the heart just stopped.'

'And you think that the same thing might have happened in this case?'

'That is not something I would be prepared to put down on paper, but purely on the pathological evidence, it's not impossible.'

'I see. Were there any signs of a struggle? Any bruising or anything like that?'

'There need not have been if my theory is correct. Some enterprising detective at the time of the Smith trial persuaded his girl friend to climb in a bath and he tried the experiment. Although she was a trained swimmer and was expecting it, she was quite unable to fight against it and for that matter, very nearly died. In this case, too, one couldn't possibly have told because she was covered in bruises anyhow.'

'Why was that?'

'I don't know whether you have ever seen modern resuscitation techniques in action, but they are pretty brutal procedures. Ribs are quite frequently broken with external cardiac massage and in fact this happened in this girl's case.'

'I suppose then, that unless something turns up with your further tests, you will be unable to give a cause of death.'

'That is so.' Golding paused to relight his pipe. 'There were, however, two other things Inspector.'

'Oh yes?'

'The first again reminds me of George Joseph Smith, who used to go in for this sort of thing. Some time ago, I would say about two to three weeks before her death, this girl was given a fairly severe beating — faint linear bruises were still present on her buttocks.'

'I see, and the second?'

'She had also been subjected to a rather savage sexual assault shortly before she died.'

Newton looked up sharply. 'The beast with two backs,' he muttered to himself.

'Did you say anything Inspector?'

'Nothing important. Are you sure?'

'Of course I'm sure,' the other man replied irritably. 'There was bruising and a small laceration in the . . . '

'Spare me the details Dr Golding, I'll take your word for it.'

★   ★   ★

The autopsy had been carried out in London and the following day Newton was driven down to Amberstead by

32

Sergeant Wainwright. He had arranged for appointments with both the Hospital Secretary and the Matron for the latter part of the morning and this gave them plenty of time to settle in at one of the local hotels.

'I'd like you to come with me to see this Secretary chap, George. It's most important that we don't put anyone's back up and it will be as well if he meets us both. Let's walk — it's a beautiful day.' George Wainwright made a face. 'Do you good, you're beginning to run to fat.' Newton punched him lightly in the stomach. 'I reckon the only exercise you ever get is in bed and if you put on much more weight, you'll lose your devastating attraction.'

★   ★   ★

St Aldhelm's was the usual hotch-potch of styles that was the trade-mark of British hospital architecture. Before the war, it had been a fever hospital and some of the original ward blocks, two storeys and built on brick stilts, were still there, although laboratories and temporary structures of one variety or another had sprung up between them. To one side a new block was going up, or it would have been more correct to say that it should have been going up. The cranes were still and a couple of bored pickets were chatting at the entrance to the site.

'Some blokes don't know when they're well off.'

'Come off it George — I can't exactly see you on a building site, you're far too fond of creature comforts.'

★ ★ ★

The Hospital Secretary got up as they were shown into his office and came forward to shake them by the hand. He was aged about sixty and although he walked with a limp and wore a hearing aid, the eyes behind the thick glasses were shrewd and Newton guessed that precious little escaped his notice and that he might well make a useful ally in the event of any difficulties.

'I fully realize that a hospital is a very

busy place and I have no doubt that enquiries of this nature will be very unpopular, but I'm afraid that the coroner is not entirely satisfied about the circumstances of Jennifer Prentice's death.'

'I see,' said the older man, although it was quite clear from his expression that he didn't see at all. 'I must say I was surprised to hear that you were coming. Like everyone else, I assumed that it was just a tragic accident — that she fainted away and slipped under the water, or something like that. Well, I for my part will do everything possible to help you in any way I can.'

'Thank you Mr Armitage. Do you know anything about the girl yourself?'

'No, not even what she looked like.' He fiddled with his pipe for a few moments. 'I don't know how much you know about hospitals, Inspector, but they are very funny places and this one is no exception. You see, there are the medical staff and all the ancillary workers on one side, the nurses on the other and then in the middle are the administrators. If you watch the television series, you might think that we were just one big happy family all working together in harmony, but you would be wrong; there is a quiet power struggle going on the whole time. I've been here a long time, longer than anyone else except Flowerdew, the night porter, and I've seen a lot of changes. Before the health service came in, the honorary consultants had a lot of power, a lot more than they have now, and some of the older ones resent the fact of their diminishing influence.'

'What about the organization of the nursing staff?'

'Well, there have been changes there too. Many of those trained under the old system feel that it is too easy nowadays for bright young women with virtually no real nursing experience to be promoted above them. They look upon them simply as administrators and feel that the art of nursing as such has become devalued — I'm not saying that they haven't got a point too. Anyway, I'd better leave you to discuss the nurses with the Matron, Miss Digby Scott.'

'Has she been here a long time?'

'About seven years. Her task was not an easy one; it never is when one has to follow an institution and Miss Massey had been matron before her for twenty-five years. Some of the sisters, used to the old régime, no doubt resented her appointment at first, but of course things have settled down a lot now.'

'I gather that Jennifer Prentice was a trainee.'

'That is correct.'

'Who is in charge of the nursing school? I thought I might see whoever it is later today.'

'Miss Fordham is the Sister Tutor; the Matron will be able to put you in touch with her.'

Roger Newton thought he detected a change in his tone of voice, but when he looked up, the other man was putting a match to his pipe.

'Well, I won't bother you any more for the time being Mr Armitage, I'm due to see the Matron in less than five minutes.'

'Let me know if there's anything further I can do for you Inspector.'

'Thank you, I will.'

★　　★　　★

The two men walked slowly towards the nurses' hostel where the Matron had her flat.

'I'll see you back in the hotel for lunch, George. Chat up the porters, they should be a mine of information.' He laughed as he saw the other man's crestfallen expression. 'It's all right George, your turn will come; I won't hog the entire supply of nubile young nurses.'

★　　★　　★

Diana Digby Scott put down the slim volume of poetry with a deep sigh and absent-mindedly drew a thin pencil line beside the verse she had been reading. It summed up with uncanny accuracy what she had been thinking; if only she could be freed from the intolerable burden that she had been forced to carry for so many years. She stared out of the window and did not move until the sharp knock at the door jerked her out of her reverie.

'Come in. Yes Winnie, what is it?'

'There's a gentleman to see you Matron; says he has an appointment.'

'That's right. Show him up will you please?'

Even though the maid could not have weighed more than at most six stone, Newton could not see how her legs managed to support her body. As he followed her up the stairs, he looked in vain for any sign of muscular action beneath the thick stockings; his index finger and thumb could have encircled her ankle with ease and there was an enormous gap between her heel and the back of her shoe. She went up sideways like a crab, grunting and muttering to herself, while her white cap slid a little lower down her wrinkled forehead at each step, until at the top it was practically touching her steel rimmed glasses.

'She's in there,' the old woman said without ceremony and before he could thank her, shuffled off with a surprising turn of speed.

Newton's first impression of the

Matron was that she was one of the most striking women he had ever seen, but almost at once he sensed something else and that was that, despite her imposing appearance, Miss Digby Scott was undoubtedly extremely nervous. Newton was well aware that policemen often had a daunting effect on people, but it was the last thing he would have expected of someone in the Matron's position — she must surely have been used to interviews.

While she poured out the coffee from the silver pot, he had a chance to look at her more closely. In many women, the elaborate starched cap would have seemed ridiculous, but in her it just added to her look of distinction. He thought he detected a hint of weariness in her grey eyes and the hand that held out his coffee was shaking, causing the cup to rattle slightly in its saucer.

'I can't disguise from you the fact that I find your visit here most disquieting, Inspector. I was given to understand that the poor girl was found dead in a locked bathroom . . . ' Her voice trailed off and she raised her shoulders ever so slightly.

'I'll try to make my enquiries as discreet as possible, Matron. The fact is, as I told Mr Armitage, the coroner is not entirely satisfied about the circumstances of Jennifer Prentice's death.'

'May I ask why?'

'I'm afraid that I'm not at liberty to say at the moment.' Newton saw the slight pursing of Miss Digby Scott's lips. He had no wish to alienate her unnecessarily, particularly as he was quite certain that the woman in front of him was desperately uneasy about something and if handled carefully might reveal why, and so he decided to relent partially. 'I can see that I'm being unfair,' he said with a smile. 'There's been an anonymous letter. It'll probably not turn out to be anything — you'd be surprised how often this sort of thing happens; it obviously gives some twisted people a kick — but of course we have to investigate it. I'd be most grateful if you'd keep this to yourself; I'm not anxious for it to get around.'

'What was the letter about?'

'I don't think it would be fair to the

dead girl or her relatives to say for the time being. I'm afraid it was rather unpleasant — these notes usually are. Can you tell me anything about Jennifer Prentice?'

'I think it would be better if you were to speak to Miss Fordham about her — she's the Sister Tutor. I'll have her sent up if you like; you might prefer to interview her here. I have to attend a meeting of the House Committee at eleven-thirty, so if you will excuse me?'

'Of course. I wonder, though, if before you go, I might ask for the use of a room? It will probably be necessary for me to see some of Jennifer Prentice's friends.'

'I'll ask Miss Fordham to see to it for you.'

Newton grinned to himself in the mirror above the fire-place; the temperature seemed to have gone up several degrees since the Matron had left. The detective wandered round the room, idly inspecting the books on the shelves. His interest quickened as he saw the comprehensive collection of English Classics and the neat row of reference books including the latest edition of *Chambers Dictionary*, a thesaurus, the *Oxford Companion to English Literature* and the *Oxford Dictionary of Quotations*.

He picked up the heavy volume and looked up 'the beast with two backs'. He was not sure exactly what he was expecting to find, certainly nothing as dramatic as the page being cut out, or the quotation being marked in pencil, but in any case, he was disappointed. Although the book was free from dust and was obviously in frequent use, there was nothing remarkable about that particular page.

Newton strolled across to the desk and picked up the slim volume which lay open by the side of the old-fashioned typewriter. He had read English himself at Oxford and had studied the Victorian poets; with one of those odd flashes of memory, he recalled that Swinburne was born the year that Queen Victoria had come to the throne. But what was the Matron of a busy hospital doing reading poetry in the middle of a Wednesday morning and Swinburne of all people with his morbid interest in corporal punishment? Surely the woman he had just met hadn't been responsible for the beating that Jennifer Prentice had received. He started to read the poem on the open page and then stopped as he saw the line drawn against the margin. Miss Digby Scott must be a very troubled woman indeed, he thought. He made an almost invisible mark with the pencil lying on the blotter and compared the two. He was near certain as he could be that the Matron had drawn the line with that pencil and probably only a few minutes earlier at that. He read the lines out aloud.

> ''From too much love of living,
> From hope and fear set free,
> We thank with brief thanksgiving
> Whatever gods may be
> That no man lives forever,
> That dead men rise up never;
> That even the weariest river,
> Winds somewhere safe to sea.''

Newton was still frowning pensively when he heard the sound of someone approaching. He moved swiftly round the desk and when the door opened, he was just getting out of his chair.

★ ★ ★

Diana Digby Scott sat bolt upright at the table in the Board Room, staring straight ahead and shutting out the abrasive voice of Fred Enright as he rode his favourite hobby-horse. Just enough was filtering through into her subconscious to enable her to incline her head at appropriate intervals and for her not to be caught totally unawares if she was asked a direct question.

Once he got going on his pet subject of the inadequacies of the accommodation in the nurses' hostel, Enright was good for at least ten minutes. Miss Digby Scott agreed with almost everything he had to say about it, but each time she saw the little man, bristling with self-importance, she fervently wished that they might have had a more prepossessing champion. His very presence on a committee was sufficient to integrate the opposition and on occasions, so outrageously did he put his points that she even found herself voting against him.

As the familiar tirade got into top gear, she found herself going over the whole business in her mind yet again. Although she realized that it was rapidly becoming an obsession with her, there was nothing she could do about it — in the last few days she hardly seemed to be able to think of anything else.

3

Newton found June Fordham, the Sister Tutor, brisk and efficient. Self assured, where the Matron had seemed nervous, she answered all his questions concisely and to the point. She wasn't bad looking in a masculine sort of way and he was willing to bet that men were not exactly an interest of hers. Newton had always been sensitive to atmosphere and there was none of the slightly electric feeling he usually noticed when interviewing young women. Although she had obviously been upset and distracted about something, he had felt it with the Matron and with the girl who had come up to see him at the Yard, but certainly not with Miss Fordham.

'Can you give me any information about Jennifer Prentice?'

The woman smiled at him confidently. 'I thought you'd be wanting that when Matron told me why you had come,

Inspector. I've brought her file along with me and I've typed out a summary for you.'

'Thanks, that's very efficient of you.'

'It was nothing — I used to be a secretary at one time and it didn't take a minute. Let's see now, she was twenty and an orphan, you know. She was highly recommended by the house mother of the place where she was brought up and did quite well at school. She was not one of our brightest nurses, but certainly a good average.'

'Did she have any relatives at all?'

'Yes, her mother is still alive, although I understand that she was illegitimate.'

'Where is the mother now?'

'In a mental hospital, I believe, but I was asked by the house mother to keep the information to myself.'

'Which department was Jennifer working in?'

'She was doing a spell in the theatres.'

'Has she been in any trouble here?'

'A bit too popular with the boys and not always in at night when she should have been, but nothing more serious than that.'

'Any health problems?'

'There's nothing on her record — she was found to be quite fit at the medical they all have at intake.' The Sister Tutor looked up from the file. 'I know it isn't really my place to ask, Inspector, but she was one of the girls in my charge and I was wondering why all these enquiries were necessary.'

'It's always the same when someone dies unexpectedly, you know. The coroner has to satisfy himself that he has discovered the correct explanation, particularly for such a tragedy as this. Then, of course, as I was telling the Matron, there was an anonymous letter.'

'You're not serious are you? Who could possibly want to write an anonymous letter to Jennifer? What did it say?'

'I'm afraid I can't tell you at the moment, but it wasn't exactly pleasant and needless to say, it makes one wonder if it was just a sick joke or whether she had any real enemies. You said she was a bit too fond of the boys; was she involved with anyone here?'

Miss Fordham got out of her chair and

paced up and down. 'I want you to understand that I'm not one to gossip, but I feel it's everyone's duty to help the police.'

Newton nodded — he had lost count of the number of times he had heard that remark in some shape or form, but who was he to complain? If people hadn't gossiped to him in the past, there would have been many occasions when he would have come up against a brick wall.

'Rumour had it that she was having an affair with the RMO and what's more, I believe he used to see her in this hostel. I see you smile, Inspector, and no doubt you're going to tell me that we live in a permissive age and so on, but remember that these girls have only just left school and we have a responsibility towards their parents to look after them. What they get up to outside the hospital is their concern, but this building is out of bounds to men and it would be impossible for discipline if it were otherwise.'

'Did you or anyone else speak to the RMO about it?'

'Well, he was never actually caught in her room. I did discuss the situation with Miss Digby Scott and she did have a word with Nurse Prentice. The situation was made much more difficult owing to the fact that the RMO is Sir Robert McFarlane's nephew.'

'Who's Sir Robert McFarlane?'

'Chairman of our Board of Governors. There's a rebuilding programme planned for the nursing school and we particularly don't want to upset him at the moment.'

'I didn't think that an individual like him had much influence in the Health Service.'

'That's where you would be wrong, Inspector. We are about to launch a public appeal for funds and Sir Robert wields a great deal of authority locally. The structure of the new block will be financed by the Department of Health, but that won't take care of lots of the amenities we are hoping for.'

'Well, thank you for your help Miss Fordham; I won't keep you any longer now. Perhaps I can call on you later if I have any other queries. One last thing, the

Matron was telling me that you would be able to arrange for me to have a room this afternoon — somewhere I can interview one or two people. As a start, I would like to see the girl who found Jennifer and also the one who was in the bath next door.'

'There'll be no difficulty about that.' The Sister Tutor looked down at her notes. 'Let me see now, Alison Carter was the one who found Jennifer; I know she'll be available this afternoon. What time would you like to start?'

'Oh, about two o'clock would suit me very well thank you. And the other girl?'

'Sarah Bennett.' She consulted the time-table again. 'Hmm — I'm afraid that's not quite so easy. She's already missed one or two of the lectures, you see, and although I could take her out of the class . . . '

Newton held up his hand. 'The last thing I want to do is cause any more disruption than is strictly necessary. Would she be free say tomorrow after-noon at the same time?'

'Yes, that would be quite all right.'

★　★　★

'Well George, and how did you get on?'

Wainwright took a long draught from his pint and wiped his mouth with the back of his hand. 'Dead loss really. Bit like the army — you don't hear much gossip about the officers in the sergeants' mess and all I heard from the porters was tittle tattle about the admin staff. They seem to know little and care less about the doctors and nurses.'

'What about the old retainer? I can't remember his name.'

'Flowerdew, you mean. He's permanently on night duty — I thought I'd have a chat with him one evening. Did you do any better sir?'

Newton raised an eyebrow at the 'sir'. 'The hospital atmosphere's good for you George; learning to show some respect at last? No, I didn't learn much either; just that there are hidden fires in that human iceberg Miss Digby Scott — she is fond of Victorian poets and is as nervous as hell about something. As for Miss Fordham, I would guess that she likes young nurses. Talking of young nurses, I want you to see what you can get out of the girl who was in the bath next to Jennifer Prentice; she's called Sarah Bennett and from what Nurse Carter told me about her when she came up to London, she's likely to be able to throw some light on Jennifer's private life — evidently they were quite good friends. I particularly want to know who the other half of the 'beast with two backs' is. See if you can find out any titbits about the Matron, the Sister Tutor and for that matter the RMO as well. You'll have to wait until you get back from London tomorrow, though, she's not available this afternoon. An interview like that should be right up your street, George.' He smiled as he saw the other man's expression. 'And George . . . go easy.'

* * *

There was undeniably something about nurses' uniforms thought Newton as Alison Carter came into the room. Perhaps it had something to do with her complete lack of make-up, which suited her flawless complexion, perhaps it was the crisply starched pinafore, which set off her figure; whatever it was, he felt a most unprofessional quickening of his pulse as he got up to greet her.

'Hello again. I thought you wouldn't mind if we had a look at the bathroom together.'

'Of course not.' She coloured slightly. 'I'm sorry I was so stupid about the 'beast with two backs' — I've looked it up since in the public library.'

'There's no reason why you should have known that particular quotation. It is the one real clue we have — any idea who the other half might have been? According to the pathologist, someone had been pretty rough with her. Miss Fordham also told me that she suspected that Jennifer brought men into her room; do you think that was true?'

This time, Alison blushed to the roots of her hair. Newton found it rather endearing; most girls seemed to him sophisticated and hard these days, that it was a relief to find someone who clearly wasn't.

'My room is next to Jennifer's and the walls aren't very thick,' she replied, looking down at the ground.

'There was someone there the night it happened, wasn't there?'

Alison looked up, surprised. 'How did you know?'

Newton decided to ignore the question. 'I want you to try to remember exactly what happened that night. Did Jennifer seem her usual self earlier in the day?'

'I didn't see much of her; you see I'm on a medical ward at the moment and she's — I mean she was — working in the theatre on Mr Pritchard's team.'

The girl looked away again and there was something in the slightly disapproving expression on her face that made him feel that an interview with this Pritchard might prove rewarding, although he decided not to question her further about him, feeling sure that she wouldn't be one to repeat rumour and gossip.

'What about after work?'

'Well, she was in supper and afterwards

I could hear her moving about in her bedroom while I was reading.'

'Let's go along there, shall we? You'll probably find it easier to remember if you're actually in the room.'

They walked down a flight of stairs and along the corridor.

'This is the one.'

'And that was Jennifer's I suppose.'

'That's right.'

Newton glanced inside. Although he hadn't really expected anything different, it was nevertheless disappointing to find the room empty. All the girl's belongings had been removed and even the mattress from the bed had gone; no doubt they would all be neatly stacked up somewhere, but any chance of learning anything useful had almost certainly disappeared for ever. Newton wondered who had been responsible and if there had been any ulterior motive behind it.

They went into Alison's room and Newton gave her an encouraging smile.

'Right you are then. Fire away.'

Alison slipped off her shoes and sat down on the bed. 'It must have been about ten o'clock and I was sitting like this reading a book. There was a lot of noise coming from the next room and I . . . I . . . '

'You heard them making love and found it embarrassing and upsetting, as I certainly would have done in your place.'

'Yes,' said Alison in a small voice. 'I behaved stupidly. I pounded on the wall and shouted at them, but as you might have expected, it made them worse. One of them hit the wall on the other side a series of terrific blows and then Jennifer opened the window and they started to make even more noise. I couldn't stand it any longer and went for a walk in the grounds.'

'Are you sure it was Jennifer who opened the window and not the man?'

'Quite sure, she shouted for me to be quiet. She didn't exactly put it that way, but that was the gist of the message.'

'So you don't think that she was being forced to do anything against her will?' He took one look at her expression and held up his hand. 'Stupid question! Have you any idea who the man was?'

'It could have been several.' He was surprised by the bitterness in her tone of voice. 'I don't think it would be fair to make a guess.'

Newton decided to let that one pass. 'What happened next?'

'I wandered around the grounds for a bit and then I met old Flowerdew, who gave me a cup of tea. We chatted for a bit and after about forty-five minutes I came back here and after undressing, went straight along to the bathroom.'

'Was everything quiet by that time?'

'Yes, Jennifer's light was out and I assumed that she had gone off to sleep.'

'Let's go along there shall we?'

They walked along the corridor and Alison paused in front of the bathroom.

'I had both my hands full with my towel and sponge bag and I pushed the door open with my foot, like this and then went inside. The engaged sign was showing on both doors and I knocked on the first one. Sarah Bennett answered and suggested that I stirred up the person next door as she had been there for a long time. I hammered on the door and when there was no reply, I got up on the chair and looked over the top.'

Newton looked around the area outside the two bathrooms. 'Is a chair usually kept out here then?'

'Now you mention it, no there isn't.' She opened the doors of both the cubicles and looked inside. 'The two chairs are usually where they are now, by the side of the baths, but there was definitely one outside that night — I couldn't be mistaken about that.'

Newton looked up at the gap above the partition. 'It must have been a pretty tight squeeze.'

'It was — I had to take my dressing-gown off.' Again the blush came. 'That's why I put Jennifer's one on when the resuscitation team arrived and of course that's how I came to discover that note.'

'I see,' said Newton pensively. 'Tell me exactly how you found Jennifer.'

'Well, she was lying flat on her back with her head under the water.' She paused for a moment and looked hard at the bath, trying to conjure up the scene again in her mind's eye. 'There was something odd,' she continued slowly, 'her heels were resting on the end of the bath on either side of the taps — I'm absolutely certain about it. It didn't strike me at the time, but thinking about it now, I don't see how she could possibly have got into that position if she'd just had a fit or fainted away.'

'The brides in the bath,' Newton said half to himself. He saw her uncomprehending look and made a sudden decision to take the girl into his confidence. 'Now you'll keep this to yourself, won't you? If Jennifer was murdered, I don't want whoever was responsible to know that we even suspect such a thing at the moment.' Alison nodded. 'Well, it was an idea the pathologist had; you see Jennifer wasn't drowned, her heart stopped suddenly, which is evidently something that may happen if water rushes unexpectedly into the mouth and nose. There was a famous murderer who was thought to have used this method.'

'If Jennifer was murdered, it must have been done by someone very thin.' Alison looked up. 'I'm sure that I could have climbed out again by standing on the edge of the bath, but getting in was really a very tight squeeze — I bruised myself quite badly — and I'm pretty skinny.'

Newton didn't think that she looked at all skinny and was about to say so, but with a great deal of effort forewent the opportunity. If he saw much more of this girl, he was going to find it progressively more difficult to maintain his detachment.

'It would also have to have been someone who was more than averagely athletic, too. Come to think of it, there's only one other person who could have done it besides you.'

'Who's that?'

'Winifred — Matron's maid.'

Alison burst into peals of laughter. 'What, that walking match-stick?'

'It's a very good suggestion. Seriously, though, let's try a little experiment.'

Newton climbed on to the chair, poked the handle of the long mop which was propped up against the wall at the side of the basin, through the gap above the door and taking careful aim, hit the knob on the bolt a smart blow. It shot into its slot with a sharp 'clunk' and with equal ease, he was able to reopen it.

He jumped off the chair. 'And for my next trick . . . '

'That's all very well, but would Jennifer have just lain in the bath doing nothing, while someone poked a mop handle down and knocked open the bolt?'

Newton looked suitably crestfallen. 'With unerring skill you have put your finger right on the flaw of the argument — Nurse Carter, you're in the wrong profession.' He reopened the door and looked at the slot more carefully and when he straightened up, all the light hearted banter had gone from his expression. 'Tell me,' he said slowly, 'if there had been something wrong with the door catch when Jennifer came in here and she was unable to shut it, what do you suppose she would have done?'

'But the door was quite definitely bolted — I have absolutely no doubt about it.'

'I know, but I just wanted to test out an

idea. What, for the sake of argument, would you have done yourself?'

'I would have used the bath in the next cubicle.'

'And if that had been occupied?'

'I would have propped the chair against the door.'

'And if there hadn't been one available either in here or immediately outside?'

'I wouldn't have bothered about it. I went to a boarding school and we weren't allowed to lock the bathroom doors — people were always wandering in and out.'

'Would it have worried Jennifer?'

Alison made a face. 'Good heavens no. It's true that a lot of girls are very self conscious in front of their own sex, much worse than boys according to my brother; 'Frailty thy name is woman' and all that.' Newton wondered if the girl knew that the quotation was referring to something much more earthy than self conscious-ness, but as she went on, was quite certain that she didn't. 'I suppose they are worried what others might think about their figure. I'm quite sure that Jennifer wouldn't have cared twopence; not only did she have a jolly good figure, but I know for a fact that she didn't mind being seen naked, indeed I believe she enjoyed it — she was always wandering around with next to nothing on. I expect she was used to it in any case — you know she was brought up in an orphanage, don't you?'

'Yes, Miss Fordham told me.'

This time, Newton was quite sure that it wasn't his imagination; Alison had reacted in just the same way as the Hospital Secretary and he was now quite sure that his feeling about the Sister Tutor had been correct.

'Good,' he said briskly, 'you've been most helpful. I'll leave you in peace now. You will keep our discussion to yourself, won't you? You know how rumours spread in a community like this.'

'You can rely on me Inspector. I won't talk to anyone about it.'

He smiled reassuringly. 'Good, I know you won't.'

★ ★ ★

When Alison had gone, Newton inspected the small metal retaining slot into which the bolt on the bathroom door fitted, with minute care. His eyes had not deceived him; whoever had repainted the door had done so without bothering to unscrew the bolt assembly. Some of the white paint had been spilt on it and it was obvious that the slot had been unscrewed very recently; not only had the paint been disturbed, but there were fresh scratches on the screws. If the murderer had removed the slot before Jennifer had had her bath, it would have been simplicity itself to replace it afterwards and then shoot the bolt across using the mop handle or something similar, in the way he had himself. No doubt the murderer — he no longer questioned the fact that it had been murder — had ensured that he or she wouldn't be disturbed by locking the door to the corridor and putting an 'out of order' notice on the handle. That was something else he must check.

Newton went back along the corridor and opposite the door of Jennifer's room he stopped and on a sudden impulse went inside. As he had expected the chest of drawers, bedside table and wardrobe were all empty and he went across to the window and looked out. The nurses' hostel was on the end of a complex of buildings and there were about twenty feet of grass before the view was obstructed by the wall which formed the perimeter of the hospital grounds. He was irresistibly reminded of a prison; the wall was constructed out of brick which had become discoloured and weathered and was topped by vicious looking pieces of broken glass.

As he turned to go, he caught sight of the scars on the wall above the bed and when he bent down and looked under it, he saw the brown envelope which was trapped between the carpet and the wainscoting. He moved the bed sideways and spent a long time studying the envelope, the wall and the carpet underneath. When eventually he left, Newton was humming quietly to himself.

4

Mr Vernon Pritchard was sitting in his office, which was on the same floor as the theatre suite, doing the crossword, when Newton went to see him later that afternoon. He was still wearing his operating kit of green shirt, trousers and cap and did not get up as the detective came into the room.

'Would you mind leaving us for a bit Angela, there's a good girl?'

The secretary who had been sitting at the desk showing a considerable amount of thigh, smiled at Newton as she went out, and the two men gave each other the sort of look that men do when they are of one mind about a pretty girl.

'Bungle the end of a chess game for a friend — eight letters?'

'Messmate,' replied Newton with only a momentary hesitation. He had done that particular crossword himself at breakfast, but saw no reason why he should admit it.

'Not bad Inspector, not bad at all.'

Newton couldn't resist the temptation to try an experiment. 'What are you like with quotations? I got stuck with one last Sunday and I haven't brought my reference books with me — I must confess that they are my weak point.'

'Try me.'

' "The beast with two backs." '

Pritchard's alert and amused expression did not slip for an instant. 'Ah, that's an easy one. It refers to 'the gross clasps of a lascivious Moor'.'

'Of course — stupid of me, I ought to have known.'

'Fifteen all?' the surgeon said with a smile. 'How about a cup of tea?'

'Thanks, I could do with one.'

Pritchard poured it out, handed it across and then settled back on the couch, looking at Newton over the top of his glasses with a twinkle in his eye.

'I can't say that I'm altogether surprised to see you, Inspector, but I must confess that it's sooner than I had anticipated. No doubt some jealous little bird has been whispering in your ear.'

Newton laughed. 'No, in fact this little bird just had a nice line in blushes. I merely asked for whom Jennifer had worked in the theatre.'

'The price of fame,' he said ruefully. 'Of course your arithmetic was impeccable, Inspector. If I don't tell you about it, I have not the slightest doubt that someone else will; you see, I knew this girl Jennifer rather well, in the Biblical sense of the word, that is. I wouldn't want you to get the wrong impression — I wasn't the first nor for that matter the last either. In point of fact, she was taken off me by the RMO of all people — he's our local Casanova.

'I can't think what Jennie saw in him — I know for a fact that he had been having an affair with one of her friends, Sarah Bennett. Her father, Geoff Bennett, was at Guy's with me and was very worried about her — he was telling me about it at the Open Day last autumn. I didn't like to tell him, but I don't think he has too much to be concerned about; that young lady knows perfectly well how to look after herself, if half the rumours about her are true. As for me, I wouldn't have minded nearly so much, if he had been a surgeon.' Pritchard saw Newton's expression and suddenly became serious. 'I know exactly what you're thinking, Inspector. How can this middle-aged lecher be joking coarsely about a young girl who has been dead less than a week? I assure you, it doesn't mean a thing — we do it amongst ourselves and sometimes forget that others can be upset by it.' He took a sip of tea. 'You'll also no doubt be wanting to know what a pretty young girl like that saw in someone like me. It's a curious place an operating theatre, Inspector. All surgeons are to some extent prima donnas and it is exciting to be surrounded by young girls wearing next to nothing, who are there for the sole purpose of answering your every command. From their point of view, too, the head of the team is a rather glamorous figure and even though I say it myself, I am not ungenerous and have plenty of money. Anyway, that's enough in the way of confessions for one afternoon. Presumably you're not satisfied about her death, otherwise you wouldn't be here.'

'No, that's right; the pathologist found it impossible to explain why she should have slipped under the water — she doesn't appear to have been an epileptic and there was no evidence of any other disease.'

'Do you think she might have committed suicide?'

'Why suicide?'

'Well, the poor girl had never had any proper family upbringing and she was always rather desperately seeking affection — probably that's why she slept around so much. You probably won't believe this, but she began to treat me like a father and that's the main reason we broke up. For the first time, I began to despise myself and saw myself as others have no doubt done for years. Jennifer was also prone to bouts of depression — like so many young people these days, she felt that life had no purpose and she was also very worried and upset about the condition of her mother who is in a mental hospital, although I never discovered exactly what was the matter with her.'

'Do you think anyone could have been jealous of her?'

'Do you mean over me?' Newton nodded. 'Well, I am married, but my wife and I have gone our own way for years. It suits us to share a house and we're really very good friends; Laura certainly wouldn't have been jealous. In any case, as I said, Jennifer and I stopped seeing one another several weeks ago.'

'Was Jennifer good at her work?'

'She wasn't fully trained you know and at that stage, nurses don't have much responsibility. If you want my candid opinion, I don't think she would ever have made a really good nurse. She was too emotional, got too upset if things went wrong. You have to develop a bit of a shell in this business Inspector — no doubt the same is true of yours.'

★ ★ ★

Some fifteen minutes later, they were interrupted by a knock and the secretary

73

put her head round the door.

'Do you want me for anything else Mr Pritchard?'

'No thank you Angela.'

The two men looked at each other again as she left the room. 'I'm afraid there's no changing the nature of the beast, Inspector.'

'I can see your difficulties — I wish I had half of them.'

Pritchard laughed. 'Well, I must go and take a shower — I'm due at my rooms in half an hour.' He shook hands and looked Newton straight in the eye. 'Find out who killed her. You may not believe this, but I happened to be in love with that girl. I don't think she felt the same way towards me, but she had known great unhappiness, you know, and I like to think that I made up for it in some ways.'

★   ★   ★

Newton walked to the end of the corridor and while he waited for the lift, looked out of the window. An ambulance was drawing up at the casualty entrance and as he watched, a still figure on a stretcher was carried in swiftly through the door. Like so many others, he had a totally unrealistic view of the sort of people who worked in hospitals. Although in the back of his mind he knew it was ridiculous, nevertheless he had put them on a pedestal and now that he was finding out that they were people in no way different from those the world over, he felt let down — yet another of his cherished illusions shattered.

'Can I help you?'

Newton turned round and saw a rather four square woman standing a few feet away. Although she could hardly have been described as attractive, he could see what Pritchard had meant; her white cotton theatre dress was semi-transparent and he could clearly make out the line of her bra and pants.

'Are you the theatre sister, by any chance?' The woman nodded, the expression in her brown eyes neutral. 'My name is Newton, Inspector Newton. Miss Fordham told me that Jennifer Prentice was working in the theatre and I came up on the off chance of being able to talk to you. You see, although we don't think that her death was necessarily other than an accident, there has been a rather unpleasant anonymous letter, which the coroner feels should be investigated.'

The theatre sister looked at him directly. 'You'd better come into my office. By the way, my name is Banks, Marjorie Banks.'

Newton usually found that people responded better if they thought that one had made a special visit to see them and he saw no reason to tell her that he had had already talked to Pritchard. He caught sight of her glancing at her watch.

'I'm sorry to have come unannounced, but I want to make my enquiries as informal as I can and to fit in with people's duties as far as possible. Can you spare me a moment?'

'I wasn't so much thinking of my duties as of my recreation; one needs to get out in the fresh air, you know, after being cooped up in there all day. It's like a hot-house for all its air conditioning; in fact I think it's worse since they installed it.' She looked up with a quizzical expression on her face. 'I suppose it's too much to hope that you're a golfer?'

'No, it isn't.'

'You have your clubs with you?'

'They're at the hotel.'

'Then you can take it that I can spare you roughly two and a half hours from the time we get on to the first tee.'

* * *

Wainwright had had to go back to London that evening to give evidence in a court case first thing on the following morning and had taken the car, so Miss Banks gave Newton a lift from the hotel to the golf course.

That journey, short though it was, was worth at least three strokes to her. It was true that she did actually start in bottom gear, but once safely in top, there she remained until they arrived. The revving and the clutch slipping were prodigious, but even that was preferable to the way she left the hotel fore-court. Newton hardly had time to close the door before

77

he was hurled backwards into his seat as the car bucketted off in a series of violent kangaroo hops, scattering an assortment of terrified old ladies and their dogs.

'The blasted thing's not pulling properly today,' she said as they crawled away from the first set of lights, clouds of grey smoke billowing from the exhaust pipe.

Newton decided to refrain from pointing out that despite the fact that it was a warm summer afternoon, the choke was pulled out to its full extent. Gradually, under the influence of the awesome vibration that was making his teeth rattle, the knob slowly retracted itself and the long suffering and much abused engine began to run with some semblance of smoothness.

Newton was feeling slightly sick as a result both of their uneven progress and the all pervading and nauseating smell of hot oil.

'You don't really think that that girl's death was an accident, do you?'

Newton looked across at her and then wished that he hadn't, because she turned to meet his gaze and narrowly missed a cyclist who was rash enough to have been using the same stretch of road.

'We do have our doubts; I wouldn't be here otherwise.'

'That's what I thought.'

Miss Banks turned towards him again, the car swerved violently and there came a sickening thud from the worn suspension as the near side front wheel mounted the kerb.

'I'm not normally a gossip Inspector,' she continued after a moment, 'but I had rather a special interest in that girl and I'd do anything to help you to find out what actually happened. Let's discuss it as we go round,' she said as they pulled up in the car park outside the club-house.

Miss Banks switched off the engine, which continued to fire at irregular intervals. She put the car into gear and let out the clutch; the long suffering vehicle gave one last despairing lurch before coming to a halt, a thin cloud of steam rising from the direction of the radiator.

'Your changing room's here. I'll see to the green fee — you can pay me back if I defeat you.'

Newton was a golfing fanatic and one of the reasons he had brought his clubs was in the hope of getting a chance to play on this course, which was one of the best in the South of England. He had played for Oxford as an undergraduate, but inevitably with lack of practice, his form had slipped a bit over the years and with it his handicap.

Miss Banks came striding out to the first tee, pulling a trolley behind her. With her white blouse, unfashionably long skirt and ankle socks, she managed to look faintly ridiculous and formidable all at the same time.

'What's your handicap?'

'A shaky five.'

'Mine's twelve. Let me see now, that means that you give me five strokes.' She consulted her card. 'Shots at the third, seventh, tenth, thirteenth and sixteenth — all right?'

'Fine. Call.'

'Tails.'

'Your honour then.'

Miss Banks advanced to the ladies' tee and took out her driver. The first hole was

504 yards long and Newton watched her preparations with interest. As he had expected, there were no frills; she took a rather wide stance, lined up carefully and with a three-quarter length swing, came in solidly behind the ball, which finished 180 yards up the fairway, just to the right of centre.

'Good shot.'

The detective teed up his ball thoughtfully. By the look of her method, Miss Banks was going to hit the ball, not particularly far, but consistently straight and if she was good around the greens, which he suspected she would be, he was going to have his work cut out. He got a good shoulder turn, but hit the ball with the face of the club slightly closed. On the hard ground, the ball seemed to go on running for ever, but there was a bit of a hook on it and he saw it disappear into the rough. Newton was unable to get any distance out of the heather and in the end, had to hole a nasty four footer to halve the hole in five.

'Look,' he said when he had replaced the flag, 'I'm enjoying this so much it seems a pity to spoil it. Why don't we have our conversation over a drink after the match?'

'I was just about to suggest the same thing myself.'

Newton won the short second with a two and when they came to the sixth tee, he was still one up.

'What's that out there?' he said, pointing to a battered looking concrete wall a quarter of a mile away in the sand hills.

'It used to be an aircraft range during the war. I wasn't here then of course, but I gather they put tanks through the course and absolutely ruined this end of it. No one goes up there much — it's said to be full of unexploded cannon shells.'

The game see-sawed back and forth with never more than two holes in it and coming to the sixteenth, they were level. Off the men's tee, the hole was 438 yards long, a very difficult par four and even though the ladies' tee was set a good forty yards further on, he doubted if she would be able to make the green in two shots. In the event, he was wrong; with the following wind, he was over the back of the green with his second, a four iron shot, while Miss Banks cut her three wood slightly and he saw her ball disappear into a steep bunker on the right, pin high.

As he walked past, Newton saw that her shot was a virtually impossible one — the ball was plugged in the sand under the face of the bunker and with the pin placing as it was, she had no green to work with. He was some forty yards ahead of her as they walked along and made no comment as he pushed his trolley round the other side of the green. His own ball was on a steep bank just over the back of the green, but as it was lying on the up-slope of a grassy bank, the shot presented no particular difficulty. As he addressed his ball, he was unable to see the bottom of the flag and walked up to get a better view. Just as he cleared the rise, he saw Miss Banks' ball appear over the side of the bunker. It landed on the edge of the green, rolled about six feet and came to a stop only a pace from the hole.

'Great shot,' he called out loudly.

Seconds later, Miss Banks emerged, brandishing her sand iron. 'Very lucky — it wasn't lying too badly, but bunker shots are not usually my strong point.'

Newton went back to his ball with a thoughtful frown on his face. 'Very interesting,' he said to himself.

Even if the shot had been on, which he doubted very much, one thing was certain and that was that an absolute shower of sand would have to have come with the ball. As it was, there had been only the merest sprinkling and that had not come out nearly far enough. It was true that he had not walked by all that close, but he was nevertheless quite certain that less than half the circumference of the ball had been showing. He was as sure as he could be under the circumstances that she had thrown it out and with it, a handful of sand. Although he got his four, Newton lost the hole when she sank the putt, having to give her a stroke, and became one down.

In normal circumstances, Newton would have done everything in his power to defeat her after that and would not have let her ball out of his sight again, but he had the strong feeling that if she wanted to win that badly, he would be much more likely to get something useful out of her if he let her do so.

In the event, he had to work quite hard to make it look convincing. The seventeenth was the last one shot hole and Miss Banks was short and to the right. Newton deliberately took the wrong club and also put it short; in fact, it was one of the best shots he had hit all day and finished exactly where he wanted it, slightly straighter than hers and some ten yards further. It was essential for him to see what sort of chip shot she played, so that he could try to match it. It was a simple enough matter to halve the hole in four, when she half topped her ball and it shot to the back of the green.

'Right. One up and one to play. Your honour.'

The eighteenth was a fairly straightforward hole. They both had good drives, but Miss Banks hit a really atrocious second, right off the toe of the club and the ball shot off almost at a right angle, into the rough. Newton saw the woman go white with rage and then give the ground a tremendous blow with her iron club, sending a divot the size of a soup plate flying up the fairway.

For some minutes Newton thought that his plan had been ruined by a lost ball, but eventually he found it himself lying absolutely unplayable, buried in the depths of a small gorse bush. When he was quite sure that she wasn't looking, he picked it out and popped it on a nearby patch of turf.

'Here you are,' he called. 'You're in luck, you've got a straight shot to the green.'

They halved the hole in five after Newton had deliberately three putted and after replacing the flag, he walked across the green with his hand outstretched and a broad grin on his face.

'Well played — what a good match! I can't say that I didn't have my chances, but my nerve failed at the critical moments. There's no doubt, though, that your last shot out of the rough was the real match winner and certainly deserved to salvage the hole.'

Miss Banks nodded her acknowledgement and as she went into the locker room, he could see that she was still beaming with pleasure.

★ ★ ★

Newton found them a couple of comfortable leather chairs in a quiet corner of the large bar lounge. At first, they just chatted about golf and went over the game they had just played, hole by hole and stroke by stroke, but almost imperceptibly he brought the conversation round to the hospital and the people who worked there. Although he started by asking her about Jennifer, it was not long before she began to tell him more and more about herself.

The story was episodic and disjointed, but when he eventually got back to his hotel, Newton brought his notes up to date and put them into some sort of order. At the time, he remembered becoming progressively more surprised at her frankness, but later realized that it was probably mainly due to the effects of three large gins and tonics on an empty stomach and after all that exercise, rather than to his sympathetic ear.

* * *

Marjorie Banks' parents were both killed in an air raid during the war, when she was twelve. She had no relatives, at least none who were prepared to look after her, and she was sent to an orphanage. Ever since she had been quite a young child, she had wanted to be a nurse and whereas many other girls living in the Home Counties would desperately have wished to get into a London teaching hospital, she was more than content when she got a place at St Aldhelm's.

The hospital atmosphere and life were all she had hoped for. For the first time, she had a measure of independence and if she was not as pretty and attractive as some of the others and did not go out much, the deep satisfaction she got out of her work more than made up for that.

She did well in her exams and within a year or two became a staff nurse.

Marjorie Banks had always been good with her fingers and it was not long before she found that working in the theatre was not only what she enjoyed doing most, but was also something at which she was naturally expert.

Vernon Pritchard was appointed to the staff when he was thirty-five. His predecessor had never really adjusted to the Health Service; before and during the war, as senior surgeon, he was a man of considerable power and influence and resented the transfer of a lot of the administrative responsibilities from the doctors to the bureaucrats. His theatre sister, Agnes Dalton, had been at the hospital even longer than him. She was getting slow and even a bit forgetful, but the two were used to one another and it was no surprise that when he retired, she went at the same time. No one was in any doubt that Marjorie Banks would be promoted and she soon settled into partnership with the new surgeon.

Vernon Pritchard appraised her, as he

appraised every woman with whom he came into contact. At first, he wrote her off as a hopeless prospect, but after working with her for several weeks, he was not so sure. It was true that she was already showing signs of becoming rather four-square, but at that time, her great attraction for him was her complete lack of sophistication.

In London, he had had his fill of brittle society women, never more so than since the time he had married one. Laura had not wanted to come down to Amberstead at all — London was where all her friends and interests lay and that was where she was determined to stay. She had money of her own and finances were no problem; they kept on their London flat and he continued to go up there for occasional weekends. Neither of them wanted children and the arrangement suited them both well enough.

When Pritchard asked Marjorie out to dinner at his flat, it never occurred to her that it was anything other than a polite gesture — the sort of invitation that many of the ward sisters received from the consultants for whom they worked.

Her first surprise came when she discovered that she was the only guest; she knew that he was married and fully expected several other people to be there. Pritchard was too old a hand to rush things. Although he found that first evening excruciatingly boring, he was not going to scare her off. Marjorie, for her part, was fully aware of his reputation and as the time approached for her to leave, was in an agony of apprehension.

When he just drove her back to the hospital, shook her hand and quickly kissed her on the cheek, she was almost sick with relief, and yet, as she lay in bed that night, she kept weaving fantasies in which the evening had quite a different ending.

In the next few weeks, Marjorie experienced feelings and emotions that she hadn't known existed. She worshipped the ground that Pritchard trod on and the realization that he had not the slightest intention of ever marrying her, did not worry her in the least — the fact that he wanted her at all was enough for her.

For the next two years, she was very happy. Pritchard was easy to work for, she knew, without any false modesty, that she was supremely good at her job and for the first time in her life, knew what it was like to be sexually fulfilled. He taught her to play golf, for which she had a natural aptitude, and even though she was aware that there were plenty of others in his life besides herself — he always seemed to find someone different to take away on holiday — he always came back to her.

The end came gradually. In her middle thirties, she began to lose her figure and put on weight. Although they continued to play golf together, their love making became less frequent and finally ceased altogether. Marjorie had had a violent temper all her life, but had always been able to control it; now, she began to snap at the nurses working on her team and was the victim of violent depressions. It was not only that she had lost Vernon Pritchard, but there was also the bitter realization that she was now too old and plain to have a chance of finding anyone else.

In the end, she got over her bad patch, helped by the arrival of June Fordham. Although different in so many ways, the two women shared a passion for golf and Marjorie was not in the least worried by the other woman's reputation. For the first time, she had someone amongst the other sisters in whom she could confide, and it gave her satisfaction to think that she was the only one to befriend June Fordham, who for some reason seemed to be generally disliked, probably because she obviously had the ear of the Matron.

Marjorie Banks noticed Jennifer Prentice the very first day she came to work in the theatre. She came through the swing doors just as the girl was tying the tapes on Vernon Pritchard's operating gown. She noticed two things almost simultaneously, firstly the look that the surgeon gave the girl and then, following his gaze, the fact that she was obviously wearing nothing under her thin cotton frock.

Marjorie Banks had not thought about Vernon Pritchard in that way for a long time and the pang of jealousy hit her with physical force, right in the pit of her stomach. She never knew how she managed to get through the list; she could not stop her hands shaking and several times she made stupid mistakes.

'Nurse Prentice, I saw how you were dressed this afternoon. You will not be coming back to work in my theatre. That will be all.'

She saw the girl's eyes fill with tears. 'But sister.'

'That will be all.'

Half an hour later, Pritchard knocked on the door.

'You know what I've come to ask, don't you Marjorie?'

She smiled wearily. 'Yes, I never could refuse you anything, could I Vernon?'

'You're a good sort, Marjorie.' He saw her look of anguish. 'You've been much more than that to me too, nobody appreciates that more than I do, but I can't help it, you know. No, I'm not trying to make feeble excuses, just attempting to give you an honest explanation. I think I'd die if I could no longer attract girls like Jennifer.'

Looking at him, she couldn't help reflecting on how kindly time had treated him and how cruelly it had dealt with her. He must have been all of fifty-five and yet he still had his figure, his vitality and above all, that extraordinary physical magnetism. She didn't blame him, or even the girl for that matter — after all, she had succumbed in much the same way.

'All right, but you won't hurt her, will you Vernon?'

He looked at her with a wry smile. 'I have a peculiar feeling that she might not be the one at risk.'

It only became clear to her what he was hinting at a few weeks later. When Marjorie discovered that Jennifer was an orphan like herself, she developed an interest in the girl that almost became an obsession. In her day-dreams, she had often prayed for a daughter and she poured all these frustrated wishes and affections on to her. She talked to her whenever possible, she took her riding on the neighbouring heathland and she persuaded June Fordham to allow her to continue working in the theatre.

It never occurred to her that all this interest might be misinterpreted until after one of their rides, Jennifer came into her room.

'You've been very kind to me, Miss Banks,' she said. 'I'm quite prepared to pay my way, you know.' She saw the other woman's look of blank amazement. 'In any way you like.'

It was several minutes before she fully realized what Jennifer was actually suggesting. The shock to her was quite shattering, particularly as she realized that her own motives for befriending the girl were suspect, though not in the way it was being taken. As for Vernon Pritchard, the poor man seemed to have fallen in love with a girl who was every bit as amoral as he had himself been over all these years.

She supposed that it was a type of poetic justice in a way, but she felt nothing but genuine sympathy for the man, particularly when Jennifer started to go out with the RMO.

'Do you know,' Pritchard said when he

was discussing it with her later, 'I'm really beginning to feel my age at last.'

★ ★ ★

Newton finished making his notes and once he had got his pipe going to his satisfaction, read them through carefully. He had written down the last few sentences of their conversation together almost verbatim and paused when he got to them, reliving the moment.

'When did Pritchard stop seeing her then?' he had asked.

'Only the night before she died, in fact; Vernon told me the following morning. Evidently she came to see him about something that was worrying her and as he put it 'one thing led to another'.'

'Did he say what it was all about?'

'No, but he didn't hold out much hope that she would come back to him.'

5

Newton had a leisurely breakfast and read through all his notes again; he was so absorbed by his thoughts that for once even the crossword was forgotten. From the picture he was building up of Jennifer Prentice, he found it impossible to reconcile on the one hand, the girl who had been accepted by the hospital for nursing training with glowing references from the foster home, with, on the other, the promiscuous young woman, who appeared to have got herself murdered.

Newton had half a mind to interview Sarah Bennett himself, but when he thought about it more carefully, realized that Wainwright would probably do the job much better. The girl did appear to have been Jennifer's one friend amongst the other nurses and would probably come up with a lot of background information if she was handled properly. She might well feel less awed by the sergeant and Newton had to admit that where young and attractive girls were concerned, Wainwright certainly had a way with him — too much of a way with him, if half the rumours circulating at the Yard were true.

Newton had taken down the address of the foster home from Miss Fordham's file and discovered, when he enquired at the reception desk, that it was only about two miles from the hotel. It was a fine morning and he decided that not only would the walk do him good, but it would give him a further chance to turn the case over in his mind.

The home was in a street on the outskirts of Amberstead. The houses were large rambling buildings, with typically Victorian architecture and most of them had untidy gardens and looked as if they were fast approaching the end of their economic life. As he approached the number he was looking for, he could see that the house was no different from its neighbours. The pointing on the brick-work had gone, an ominous looking crack was visible on one of the side walls and many of the slates were either loose or missing.

A large unkempt man in his middle thirties and with a mass of unruly ginger hair was digging a vegetable patch at the side.

Newton leaned over the hedge. 'Excuse me. Is this the Foster Home?'

The man straightened slowly, wiped his hand on the back of his jeans and stuck the spade into the ground with unnecessary force. His attitude and expression were not exactly aggressive, but they were not exactly friendly either and Newton paused for a moment, considering the best approach. When the man nodded in answer to his question, he quickly decided that it would be more tactful to assume that he was in charge of the Home, even if he was just a jobbing gardener, rather than make the mistake the other way round.

'Good. I wonder if you could spare me a moment. I am a police officer and I was wondering if you could give me some information about Jennifer Prentice.'

Newton was watching the other man

carefully and although it was almost instantly extinguished, he was sure that he hadn't imagined the look of surprise and alarm on his face. However, he seemed to come to a sudden decision and as he walked forward, he was smiling broadly.

'Come in. I could do with a break.' He held out a large freckled hand. My name's Bradley. I run this place with my wife Barbara — she's out at the shops at the moment, but she shouldn't be long. All the children are at school.'

They sat down at the kitchen table, each with a glass of beer.

'Have you been here long?'

'No, only three years.'

'Then you probably didn't know Jennifer Prentice all that well.'

'Oh yes, we knew her all right.' He saw that Newton had noticed his change of expression. 'Yes, Barbara and I were of course terribly upset when the Matron rang us up to tell us about Jennifer's death. It wasn't just an accident was it?'

'What makes you ask that?'

'Well, in the first place, I don't suppose you'd be here if it had been and Barbara and I were always saying that one day that girl would come to a sticky end.'

'Tell me about her.'

'Barbara and I were both psychiatric social workers — that's how we came to meet each other — but unfortunately, about five years ago she contracted TB very badly. She had to have part of one lung removed and when she was through the convalescent period, we decided to look for a quieter job out of London, at least until she had got her strength back completely. Barbara had had experience with disturbed adolescent girls and when we saw the post advertised, we applied and were delighted to get it. We look after eight girls here, taking them when they are old enough to go to secondary school and keeping them until they get jobs and are able to be independent or until they reach the age of eighteen.

'I suppose Jennifer must have been about sixteen when we arrived here; she was in fact the most senior girl and it was immediately obvious that she was going to be a bit of a handful, to say the least of it. We had only been here about three months when she stayed out all night following some party in the town. Initially, I left it to Barbara to talk to her, but she was very rude and so I had a word with her too. I can't remember exactly what I said, but no doubt it was the usual talking-to one hands out in these circumstances — there were some reasonable rules we expected her to follow, we had a responsibility for her, there were dangers to her if she behaved like that, and so on.

'She listened to what I had to say without interrupting or trying to make excuses and then quite calmly said; 'aren't you going to beat me?' I was flabbergasted and pointed out that I didn't think that beating people was the answer to anything. 'Oh,' she replied, 'Mr and Mrs Manson always used to.''

'Presumably they were the people who ran this place before you.'

'That's right.'

'Why did they leave?'

'You might well ask. Their marriage broke up and it didn't take me long to find out why. Inevitably, in any family, parents and their children see each other naked from time to time, but with Jennifer, it was clearly no accident. She just happened to come out of the bathroom with nothing on when I was walking by, she just happened to slip off the top of her bikini when she was sunbathing outside the study where I was working — you can imagine the sort of thing. Barbara saw what she was up to, of course, and was able to put a stop to it before things got out of control. I'm not saying we didn't have our ups and downs with her afterwards, but she did settle down quite a lot.'

'You were saying that the Manson's marriage broke up — I presume from what you were saying that it was on account of Jennifer.'

'Yes, I think so. You see ... ' He stopped speaking abruptly at the sound of the front door being opened and once more, Newton had the impression that the man was distinctly uneasy. 'That'll be Barbara back from the shops — she'll be able to tell you more about it.' He got to his feet and went to the door. 'Hello dear, there's an Inspector Newton here; he's come to make some enquiries about Jennifer.'

Barbara Bradley was painfully thin and even though the June morning was only pleasantly warm, there was an unhealthy flush on her cheeks and she kept wiping the perspiration from her forehead with her handkerchief.

'I hope I'm not disturbing you too much,' said Newton when Bradley had gone back to the garden.

'No, I need to sit down for a bit anyway; I still have to take things rather slowly.'

The woman listened in silence while Newton briefly explained why he was there and then had a paroxysm of coughing, which seemed to leave her exhausted.

'I'd be glad to help in any way I can, Inspector. How much did Derek tell you about her?'

When he had finished giving her a résumé, Barbara Bradley sat for a long time staring at the detective across the table.

'The Matron told me that it was an accident, but I hardly imagine that you would have come out here unless there was something suspicious about Jennifer's death.'

'Oh, I wouldn't say that — the coroner just wants to satisfy himself completely about the circumstances. It's always the same after any unusual accident.'

Newton could see straight away that he hadn't convinced her.

'Naturally this whole business came as a great shock to me,' she said, 'but I can't say I was altogether surprised to hear that something had happened to her.'

'What makes you say that?'

'You'll treat what I have to say in complete confidence, won't you Inspector? Most of what I have to tell you came from Jennifer herself and I wouldn't want to spread unfounded rumours, but whatever else she was, that girl wasn't a liar, as I discovered to my cost.'

Now whatever is that supposed to mean, thought Newton, having the intuitive feeling that he would rather not know what this ravaged looking woman was going to tell him. This was the part of his job that he liked least of all, but he forced himself to give her a reassurring smile.

'Of course.'

'Well, I only discovered most of the facts about Jennifer when we had been here about a year, but I'll try to put them in some sort of order for you.

'Jennifer was illegitimate and her mother, who lived in the town here, if not exactly a prostitute, was pretty free with her favours. She evidently had one lover after another, most of whom, like her, drank heavily. You can imagine what sort of environment for a young child that was and you'll not be surprised to hear that it eventually occurred to one of those brutes that Jennifer was both growing up and looking much more attractive than her mother. The poor little thing was only twelve at the time and was sent here as being in need of care and protection, when it was discovered.

'There seemed to have been something about Jennifer that brought out the worst in men. It wasn't long before Manson took over where her 'stepfather' had left off. Mrs Manson had her suspicions, but was unwilling to believe them until one day, Jennifer, who was being punished for some offence, told her to her face — that's when the beatings started. That first time, Mrs Manson went on until Jennifer 'admitted' that she had made it all up, but after that they were frequent occurrences. Jennifer even told me that she used to provoke them into hitting her — I genuinely believe that she actually enjoyed it.

'In the end, the Board got to hear about some of the things that were going on here — Jennifer wasn't the only one to be treated badly — and the Mansons were kicked out. It's difficult to believe that things like that could still be going on in this day and age, but I assure you they did. I must confess that when I first heard about all this from Jennifer, I thought she was probably making a lot of it up, but one of the other girls here confirmed most of it and more recently I heard more about the Mansons from one of the members of the Board, a woman with whom we play bridge occasionally.

'We hadn't been here long before Jennifer began to get up to her tricks with Derek. You never saw her, did you Inspector?'

'No, I didn't.'

Mrs Bradley went into the next room and came back with a photograph album.

'Jennifer was really most attractive. This was taken when we all went down to Brighton for the day.'

Newton looked at the snap of the group on the beach and it was immediately obvious which girl was Jennifer. She stood out like a beacon; she was a woman, and a very pert and attractive one at that, amongst a collection of children.

'Well, one day I told her off about something or other and she taunted me with the fact that she was sleeping with Derek. Although I didn't believe her for one instant, she couldn't have found anything worse to say to me. At that time, I knew virtually nothing about her past history and I still hadn't recovered from what the tuberculosis had done to me. I didn't always look like this, you know, and

I was only too painfully aware that not only my looks had gone, but as the result of peritonitis, I would never be able to have children.

'I don't know where I found the strength to deal with it; perhaps it was just luck that I hit on the right thing to say. I remember that I was quite calm and gave no hint that I had any doubts about my husband. I told her that she must be very unhappy to have said things like that, that we had no intention of rejecting her and so on.'

'What was her reaction?'

'Floods of tears and self recrimination — how could she have said such horrid things when we had both been so kind to her? She promised not to say anything like it again and it was then that she told me about all the things that had happened to her in her early life. I never had any real trouble with her after that. She got on quite well at school, managed a few 'O' levels and I pulled a few strings to get her into St Aldhelm's — Sir Robert McFarlane is both chairman of our Board and that of the hospital. He donated this house originally and takes a great interest in the girls here, so when I told him I thought that Jennifer would make a good nurse, there was no great difficulty, particularly when he heard about all the trouble she had had with the Mansons. Sir Robert seemed to think that if the Board had been more on its toes, it would have discovered what was going on much earlier. Anyway, I thought that the supervision and discipline that Jennifer would get as a trainee nurse would allow her to mature and I hoped that in time she would learn some responsibility. It seems that I was wrong.'

'I'm quite sure that you have nothing to reproach yourself with. No one could have done more for her. What happened to her mother?'

'Didn't I tell you? She's in the Arlington mental hospital; she must have been there for a good five years now. I went to see her once, but I'm afraid that the visit was not a success.'

Newton could see that the woman was tired and got to his feet.

'Thank you so much Mrs Bradley,

you've been most helpful.'

She saw him to the front door.

'Good-bye Inspector.' She started to close the door and then, with sudden decision, called after him. 'Oh, Inspector!'

Newton turned to face her again, once more being struck by the unnatural brightness of her eyes and the hectic flush on her cheeks.

'Yes.'

'You know that I told you that Jennifer wasn't a liar? Well, she wasn't lying about my husband either; she had been sleeping with Derek all along and continued to do so after she left here — I only found out a few weeks ago.'

Newton saw the tears start to her eyes, then the door was slammed shut and he was left standing uncertainly half-way down the path. He took a pace or two back towards the house, then changed his mind and strode rapidly away. As he went along the pavement, he looked over the hedge, but Bradley was nowhere to be seen.

★ ★ ★

Newton took a taxi out to the Arlington mental hospital that afternoon. Some of the ward blocks were very similar in design to those at St Aldhelm's, but were much more widely dispersed in the very large grounds, which must have covered a good square mile.

Dr McAlister, the Physician Superintendent, waved him to a chair in his office and picked up the buff folder lying on his desk.

'I'm sure you'll be wanting to see Mrs Prentice yourself, but I'm afraid you won't be able to get much information out of her — she's very disturbed.'

'What's the matter with her?'

'She's got Huntington's Chorea.'

'Whatever's that?'

'One of the most tragic diseases we have to deal with. It's an inherited disorder, characterized by involuntary movements and mental changes. These unfortunate patients really do look mad in the lay sense of the term — they twitch and jerk and in the later stages are very psychologically disturbed as well. There's good evidence that people with this disease were burned to death as witches in the distant past. Being a genetic disorder, there is unfortunately no curative treatment; one can only attempt to deal with some of the worst symptoms by the use of drugs. One particular reason why it is so tragic is that it does not usually manifest itself until after the thirties or forties, long after the potential sufferer has had to make a decision about marriage and having children.'

'Is there no way of predicting whether or not someone is going to get it?'

'No, that's just the point. The condition is inherited by what is called a dominant gene, which means that any child of an affected parent stands a fifty fifty chance of getting it and we have no means of telling in advance. You can see that as the disease does not declare itself sometimes until middle age, the wretched person has to wait on tenterhooks for many years.

'Of course it is the individual's own decision, but it is my usual advice that the children of these people should not marry and if they do, should certainly not have children.'

'I see. Do you happen to know if Jennifer knew of her mother's diagnosis?'

'Yes, only too well — I told her myself. Let's see now.' He flicked through the notes. 'Yes, that's right, I saw her with her foster mother nearly three years ago, when she was sixteen. Terrible though it was, I felt I had to tell her before she got seriously involved with a boy-friend and started to think about marriage.'

'How did she take it?'

'She didn't say very much at the time, just asked a few questions which clearly showed that she had taken it all in. Of course, children like her, who have had disturbed upbringings and are continually being shifted from one home to another, develop a pretty thick skin. Incidentally, I didn't take to her foster mother at all — Mrs Manson her name was; she seemed to me to be a very hard and unsympathetic type of woman.'

'Is there any chance that Jennifer could have actually been suffering from the disease at the time of her death?'

'It's true that I have heard of it appearing in the teens, even in early childhood, but it must be very unusual. What made you think of it?'

'Well, even making every allowance for her terrible upbringing, the more enquiries I make, the more disturbed does she appear to have been.'

'In what way?'

'Even for these days, she seems to have been remarkably promiscuous and had strong masochistic tendencies as well.'

McAlister leafed through the notes and ran his finger down the first page.

'Now that's very interesting; you see that's just how Mrs Prentice's illness started off. Jennifer was born when she was only nineteen and according to the social worker's report, even then she was promiscuous in her behaviour. It's not at all uncommon for the psychiatric disturbance to precede the involuntary movements by several years. Has anyone commented on Jennifer having been unusually fidgety?'

'Not that I can recall, but then of course I haven't asked specifically.'

'You know Inspector, you may well be

right, but there's no way of proving it now.'

'Wouldn't the pathologist who did the autopsy be able to tell?'

'I'm no great expert on that side of things, but I doubt it. You'll have to ask him.'

'Do you happen to know if Jennifer saw her mother recently?'

'Yes. She used to come every few months, but the last time, which must be about six months ago now, I advised her to stop coming. Mrs Prentice did not recognize her and it seemed to me that it was distressing the poor wee girl unnecessarily. Now, if you'll forgive me, I have to go to a meeting just now.' He pressed the buzzer on his desk. 'I'll get Mr Johnson, one of the senior nurses, to take you along.'

★   ★   ★

Newton followed the male nurse down what seemed an endless series of corridors. The man obviously kept taking short cuts, locking and unlocking doors with keys from the enormous bunch he kept in his pocket, but even so, Newton reckoned that they must have walked nearly a mile before eventually they reached the right ward.

'You wait here in sister's office, sir, and I'll get Mrs Prentice for you. I don't think you'll have any problems with her, but if you do, just press that bell there and I'll be right in.'

Newton had seen from the records that Mrs Prentice was only thirty-eight, but the figure that came into the room looked at least sixty, although it was still just possible to see that she must have been quite pretty at one time. When she sat down in the chair, she seemed in imminent danger of falling off; the poor woman was quite incapable of keeping still. She was continually twisting her fingers and her facial expression was constantly distorted by grimaces and every few seconds, animal grunts issued from her constantly moving lips.

The detective spent five minutes trying to talk to her, but it was a hopeless task. In all that time, he was able to decipher only one sentence, which the hapless woman kept repeating over and over again: 'Jennifer's a nurse . . . Jennifer's a nurse.'

Mr Johnson came back in immediately in response to Newton's ring.

'It's very distressing, isn't it?' he said, seeing the Inspector's expression. 'It's terrible to see these people getting steadily worse and not being able to do a thing about it.' He shook his head dolefully. 'Come on Annie, there's a good girl.'

The woman shambled out, hitting the frame of the door a violent blow as a sudden spasm carried her sideways.

★ ★ ★

Although it was a good five miles back to the hotel, Newton felt in the mood for a long walk. Perhaps, he thought, Jennifer's death had been for the best after all; he was quite sure in his own mind that she did have the disease and at least she had gone quickly and painlessly. He tried imagine what it must have been like for a pretty young girl to have seen her mother reduced to a jerking puppet and to have known full well that the same thing might happen to her in a few short years. Even apart from whatever effects the disease might have had on her, it was little wonder she had been promiscuous; no doubt she was continually seeking reassurance that she was still attractive and desirable.

What would her thoughts have been too, if she had realized that she was actually getting the first symptoms and still had enough insight to take in the implications? Was it possible, after all, that she had committed suicide? If so, what a way to do it, and surely she wouldn't have gone to the lengths of writing anonymous letters to herself; in any case, too, there was the evidence that he had found in both the bathroom and her bedroom. No, that idea was impossible.

By the time he got back to the hotel, it was about five o'clock, but although the Rover was in the car park, there was no sign of Wainwright and Newton presumed that he was still up at the hospital. He put a call through to Golding and contrary to what McAlister had said, the pathologist seemed to be fairly confident that he would be able to say if the earliest stages of Huntington's Chorea were present within the next forty-eight hours. Newton didn't understand the technicalities, but the man said something about making frozen sections. The detective also got through to the Yard and was well pleased with the information he received — now there was something else that they could get to work on.

Although Newton was extremely intrigued by the case, he was, at the same time, thoroughly depressed by it. If Jennifer really had had the disease, then her disturbed behaviour was easy enough to explain, but what really depressed him was the number of men involved with her, none of whom seemed capable of exercising even the elements of self control. It wasn't even as if any of them were young boys, who might not have been expected to know better — they were doctors and foster parents, who were in positions of trust and responsibility.

For once, he regretted not being able to discuss it with someone — he even found himself missing Wainwright — and to take his mind off it, went out to the golf course in the car and spent a couple of hours on the practice ground. At first, he could not prevent himself from lashing at the ball and sent shot after shot in low raking hooks far away to the left, but gradually he relaxed and his rhythm returned. As the ball began to fly off, straight as a die, shining white against the brilliant blue sky, he felt his tension subsiding and when he got back to the hotel and had had a couple of pints of beer, he felt tired, but his usual good humour had returned.

6

George Wainwright was in a vile temper as he returned to Amberstead after the court hearing. Although in the back of his mind, he realized that he was driving both aggressively and dangerously, it required a near head-on collision when he overtook a lorry on a blind corner, to bring him to his senses. There was no possible excuse for his action and the incident acted on him like a bucket of cold water over the head.

He pulled into the next lay-by and walked up and down the road for ten minutes, quite literally shaking at the thought of what an accident under these circumstances would have meant to his career. He prided himself on his driving skill and had lost count of the number of warnings he had issued under similar circumstances, when he had been in the uniform branch on road patrol.

The trouble had been that Wainwright

knew that Armstrong was guilty, the defence counsel knew it and for that matter, he was quite certain that the Judge knew it as well, but the jury had come to quite a different conclusion. What riled him particularly, though, was not that a guilty man had got off — that had happened often enough before and doubtless would again — but the suggestion that he had planted the drugs himself and the fact that the jury obviously believed it.

'Tell me, Sergeant, am I correct in believing that my client was tried on another charge two years ago?' the defence counsel had said.

'Yes sir,' he had replied heavily, knowing what was coming.

'Would you tell the jury what this charge was?'

'Stealing a car, sir.'

'And who was the officer who made the arrest?'

'I did.'

'I see.' He had paused dramatically and raised his eyebrows in a gesture that said more than if he had spelled it out in words of one syllable. 'And what was the verdict?'

'He was found not guilty.'

The barrister did not in so many words accuse him of having been prejudiced against Armstrong or of having planted the drugs, but the implications were there, none the less and Wainwright was only partially successful in controlling his temper. The prosecuting counsel had done his best to protect him, but Armstrong had obviously been well briefed and was in perfect control of himself.

The man stuck to his story that he had no idea how the drugs came to be in his room; he pointed out that there were eight bed sitting rooms in the house and that people were always coming in and going out, and when he was asked point blank if he was accusing Wainwright of having planted them, he denied it with just the right blend of injured innocence and surprise that such a suggestion should have been made. As he left the witness box, Wainwright knew that the man had got away with it again and could feel the blood pounding in his ears as Armstrong looked across at him, a half smile of triumph on his face.

★ ★ ★

By the time he got back into the car, Wainwright had calmed down, realizing that once he started to allow himself to be needled so easily by yobs like Armstrong, he might as well pack it all in. He drove the rest of the way with meticulous care and his spirits began to lift after he had had a slice of cake and a cup of tea at a café on the outskirts of Amberstead.

He felt even better an hour later, when Sarah Bennett came into the room that Miss Fordham had made available for them. In a few years' time, he reckoned that she would almost certainly run to fat, but now, to his eyes, she could best be described as cuddly and he liked his girls well covered.

As the girl settled down in her chair, it was obvious that she was completely at ease.

'Sorry I'm so late,' Wainwright said, 'I got held up in London.'

'It couldn't have suited me better,' the girl replied in her rather breathless voice. 'I was allowed out of the first class of the afternoon because of this interview and now I've managed to escape the anatomy test. I'm absolutely hopeless at it anyhow and to make matters worse I hadn't done any revision. The interview won't be over too quickly, will it Sergeant?'

'I think I can guarantee that,' replied Wainwright with a smile. 'There are lots of questions I want to ask you Miss Bennett.'

'Not too many I hope Sergeant.'

Wainwright cleared his throat and swallowed painfully. 'You're a very important witness you see, and we want to find out exactly what happened.'

'You mean it might not have been an accident?'

'We always have to consider every possibility.'

Sarah Bennett's cornflower blue eyes opened wide. 'You don't mean that she might have been murdered with me in the bath next door?' She gave a little shiver of excited horror. 'How creepy can you get?'

'No, of course not.'

'Well, if it had been true, it wouldn't have surprised me all that much.'

'Why? Did she have a lot of enemies?'

'No special ones that I can think of, but she wasn't exactly popular. I quite liked her myself, but she was a bit too moody for most people's taste. I often told her, though, that she would come to a sticky end one day.'

'Whatever made you say that?'

'Well, I know I'm not one to talk, but I reckoned she was a bit too free and easy for her own safety, a bit kinky too. Perhaps it was because she was brought up in an orphanage.'

'In what way kinky?'

'Well, we went bathing once to a lake — it's about five miles from here — and we were both changing in the boat-house. Jennifer never thought anything of walking about with nothing on and when she turned her back to me, I was absolutely staggered; you never saw such a sight, her backside was black and blue. 'Whatever's happened to you, Jennifer?' I said. She looked over her shoulder at me in ever such a funny way. 'Oh, I just fell off my bike the other day.' 'Come off it,' I said, 'I'm not that stupid, I can see the weals. Who did it to you?''

'Did you ever find out?'

'No, she just told me to mind my own business. The funny thing is, though, that I'm sure she meant me to see it — it must have given her some sort of kick. She obviously enjoyed talking about that sort of thing, too; she was always telling me about the beatings she used to get at her foster home. I must confess, that at one time I thought she made half of them up, but after seeing what someone had actually done to her, I wasn't so sure. She used to tell me that it was better to be beaten than to be ignored; at least that showed that someone was taking an interest in her. Rather pathetic really, don't you think?'

'What sort of blokes did she used to go out with?'

'Well, the latest one's rather a nasty piece of work; he could easily have been the one who hit her, but I know for a fact that he didn't, because he hasn't been here that long.'

'Who's he?'

'Ian Moore, the RMO. He's the senior resident and thinks he owns the place.'

'Did you ever go out with him yourself?'

'No thank you; I don't fancy the caveman approach. You should have heard some of the noises that used to come out of Jennifer's bedroom. She was taking the most frightful risk — the nurses' home is strictly out of bounds to doctors, or any men for that matter.'

'Isn't that rather out of date?'

'Oh, it's all done with our best interests at heart, you know,' she said with heavy sarcasm. 'To protect us from predatory males.'

'Well, I've no doubt that Inspector Newton will be wanting to interview this Moore.'

'He'll be lucky. Hadn't you heard — he was taken ill a few days ago; I believe he's quite bad.'

'I'm sorry to hear that; what's the

matter with him?'

'I don't know, but he was moved to the intensive care unit this afternoon.'

'Did you know any of her other boy-friends?'

'In point of fact, no. She was always ready enough to tell me what she was getting up to, but not with whom she did the getting, if you know what I mean. There were rumours about her and Pritchard, but then in a place like this, there are rumours about everyone.'

'Who's Pritchard?'

'One of the surgeons — Jennifer was working on his team when she died. I think he must have fixed it up specially — student nurses don't usually stay in the theatre for so long; she must have been there all of three months.'

'Did Jennifer have any girl-friends apart from you?'

'Not really. She was always a bit suspicious of people who were nice to her — she always assumed that they had some ulterior motive. I think that's one of the reasons why we got on so well; I always used to tell her exactly what I thought.'

'What about Alison Carter? She had one of the rooms next door to Jennifer, didn't she? Weren't they friendly?'

'Good Lord no. Alison didn't approve of the way Jennifer behaved — she's far too pi for that.'

Wainwright was surprised at the venom in her voice. 'Don't you like her either then?'

Sarah made a face. 'I suppose she's all right — bit too much of a goody-goody for my taste. She always comes top in the tests, never does anything she shouldn't — you know the sort of person I mean.' She giggled and looked across the desk at him. 'We've got plans for Alison at the party after we take our exams; it was Jennifer's idea originally, but it's much too good to waste.'

'What sort of plans?'

'That would be telling, wouldn't it? But I guarantee that it'll wash some of the starch out of her. I must say this for her, though, she was jolly good when she found Jennifer. She was in there like a flash, doing artificial respiration and all that, while I just screamed the place down. I can tell you, I got the shock of a life-time when I looked over the partition and saw Jennifer's face under the water; I still dream about it. Still, we can't all be perfect.'

'No, thank goodness,' Wainwright replied, giving her a look. 'That would make life far too dull. What's it really like here? What about those in authority?'

'Oh, they're not too bad really. There's the odd frustrated spinster, who's jealous of anyone young and pretty and then there are the ones like Miss Fordham, who are a bit bent.'

'What's wrong with her?'

'Well, as you can imagine, nursing, like the women's forces, attracts some people who are more than a little interested in their own sex. I've never heard that she's actually ever done anything, but she definitely likes to have a look.'

'How do you mean?'

'She runs the nurses' sick bay, as well as administering the teaching and do you know, when I was first here, I went to see the RMO because I had a sore throat and she told me to strip off completely. I was pretty dumb in those days and did so — you should have seen her eyes, they practically came out on stalks. The funny thing was, though, that it turned out quite well for me in the end; the RMO thought I was doing it for his benefit and asked me out. I've never understood how he managed to avoid being struck off. I must say this for Ian Moore; he had hardly been appointed before he saw what she was up to and complained to the Matron — that soon settled her hash. She's not a bad sort, though, old Fordham; at least she's human, which is more than can be said for Eskimo Nell.'

'Eskimo who?'

'Nell. It's our name for the Matron — the ice queen herself, Miss Diana Digby Scott. Do you know, rumour has it that she wears her uniform in bed.'

'What a terrible lot you are! I feel quite sorry for the poor woman.'

'You wouldn't if you'd met her. Going into her room is like entering a church — whenever I look at her, I expect to see a halo sitting above her head.'

'No doubt she sees a devil with a long forked tail perched on your shoulder. What time do you have to be in at night?'

'Eleven.'

'Isn't that rather a drag?'

'You don't suppose we stick to that, do you? Old Flowerdew on the gate is on our side and anyhow, we can always climb in.'

'What, over the wall at the back? What about the glass?'

'A section of that was removed years ago; there are special cracks in the brick-work too. It's a piece of cake.'

'What do you do with yourself when you have time off? This seems rather a one-horse sort of area.'

'Oh, it's not so bad, you know. I go riding and there's a fellow who lives near here, who's got a boat and some of us go water skiing on the lake — you know, the one I told you about where I went swimming with Jennifer.'

'That sounds fun.'

The girl looked at him archly. 'It is. I could show you if you like.'

Wainwright was sorely tempted, but if

Newton ever found out — and with the sort of gossips that always existed in closed communities like hospitals, that was inevitable — he would be sent packing and quite rightly too. Sarah Bennett was, after all, very close to the crime and a suspect herself, even though a very unlikely one.

'I don't somehow think that would be very wise,' he said with a laugh, trying to keep it light. 'I might forget that I was on duty.'

'But Sergeant, that was the whole idea.'

★ ★ ★

Wainwright wandered back to the hotel in the late afternoon sunshine, feeling a sense of virtue that came partly from having conducted a successful interview, but even more from having resisted a strong temptation. His instincts about girls were seldom wrong and he had known within minutes of seeing Sarah Bennett that she was ripe for the plucking and that it would be an experience to remember — she was most certainly not just a tease. Once or twice in the past he had seen what had happened to police-men who mixed business with pleasure and he wasn't going to make that mistake himself. He also had enough insight to realize that girls like Sarah Bennett, whose whole manner and appearance shouted middle class, were not for him.

At the hotel, he found a note from Newton to say that he had gone to the golf course and he settled down to wait in the lounge, but when he saw the Rover through the window, he suddenly decided that he couldn't face the inevitable long drawn out discussion of the case and slipped out of the side entrance.

On the way down to the town, he had to pass the main entrance of the hospital and the elderly man in uniform standing at the gate smiled at him.

'Hello,' he said. 'My name's Flower-dew. You must be Sergeant Wainwright.'

'How did you know that?'

'Oh, people tell me things, you know.'

Wainwright hadn't escaped from Newton to spend the evening talking to someone else about the case, but this was too good an opportunity to miss. In the event, the old man did little more than confirm most of the things that Sarah Bennett had told him, but he did let slip one piece of information about Alison Carter that made him smile to himself; Newton was always taking the Micky out of him, now he would have some ammunition of his own with which to get some of his own back.

'Is there anything to do in this place in the evenings?' he said as he turned to leave.

'Well, there are a couple of cinemas, but perhaps you have in mind something a bit more out of the way.'

'Such as what, for example?'

Flowerdew looked round to make sure that no one was within earshot and then whispered something in his ear.

Wainwright was chuckling to himself as he walked away. 'The old devil,' he said to himself. Perhaps the day wouldn't end on a note of anti-climax after all.

7

Newton was drinking his second cup of coffee and was half-way through the crossword when Wainwright came down to breakfast.

'Where did you get to last night then, George? Sampling the local talent? I was expecting to see you at supper time. And you can take that self-satisfied expression off your face. Well, let's have it, what did you discover when you interviewed Sarah Bennett?'

'Have a heart, sir. Let me get outside some bacon and eggs and then I'll tell you.'

Ten minutes later, Newton gave a grunt of satisfaction. 'Assail,' he said decisively.

'What was that, sir?'

'Attack gives a fool trouble, ass-ail, the last clue in my crossword. Right now, you've had long enough to get over your nocturnal excesses. Make it concise.'

Newton listened in complete silence

while Wainwright gave him a précis of the information he had gleaned from Sarah Bennett. When he had finished, the Inspector nodded his head.

'Well done George, well done indeed. It's nice to see that you can keep your mind on your work whatever the distractions.'

'Did you make out all right with Nurse Carter, sir?'

Newton sighed deeply. 'There are times, George, when you over-step the bounds of propriety and that is one of them. Some of us are capable of exercising some degree of self control, you know. Now, let's get down to business.'

Newton opened his notebook and gave Wainwright a résumé of his interviews with the Matron, Miss Fordham, Nurse Carter, Vernon Pritchard and Sister Banks, as well as an account of his visit to the foster home and mental hospital.

'Now George, after hearing all that, what do you think? Was that ghoul Golding right and was Jennifer Prentice murdered, could it have been suicide or was it just an accident?'

'She certainly seems to have been somewhat free with her favours and catholic in her tastes, but we haven't got anything really solid to go on apart from that anonymous letter and what you found in the bathroom.'

'George, you're developing a positively literary turn of phrase. Yes, what you say is true, but even though it is conceivable that it was an accident after all and the letter, the work of someone sick, it will do no harm to review what we have learned to date. Let's deal with the anonymous note first, or rather the envelope in which it probably came.'

'What envelope? I thought that Nurse Carter just found the piece of paper in the dressing-gown pocket.'

'So she did, George, but I found a typewritten envelope addressed to Jennifer Prentice tucked in between the carpet and the wainscot in her bedroom and there was something very odd about it.'

'Oh, in what way?'

'Mainly that it was there at all. The room had obviously been cleaned up thoroughly and I find it difficult to believe that it wouldn't have been removed, particularly as I'm sure that the carpet had been vacuumed after Jennifer's death.'

'How did you know that?'

'In the first place, I asked the maid and secondly, Jennifer had bashed the wall with the base of the bedside lamp that night — she was trying to shut Alison Carter up — and there were quite a few holes in the wall where the plaster had been knocked out. Although I found traces of it on the lamp, there was nothing on the carpet at all.'

'You're suggesting that the envelope was put there later?'

'It certainly looks like it. I sent it up to the Yard and Wells tells me that it was typed on a twenty-year-old Imperial and that it was done by an amateur.'

Wainwright groaned. 'I suppose I now have to tramp around the hospital looking for an old Imperial type-writer.'

Newton grinned. 'At least you are spared that labour, my dear George. When I was alone in Miss Digby Scott's room the day before yesterday, what should I happen to notice?'

'An antique Imperial type-writer.'

'Correct in one and a quick visit to the porter's lodge proved that the letters the Matron sent down to the post yesterday were typed on the same machine as the anonymous letter.'

'Why are you so sure that the anonymous note was in an envelope?'

'Because Jennifer received another one a few days earlier, thought Alison Carter had sent it and brandished a similar envelope in front of her nose.'

'Seems a bit too easy to me.'

'George, we are on precisely the same wavelength; either Miss Digby Scott is an extremely careless killer — and from my one meeting with her, she didn't strike me at all as being a careless person — or there is a plot to point the finger of suspicion at her. The envelopes are not exactly subtle, but I am much more impressed by the coincidence of her liking for Swinburne and the fact that, according to the Bradleys and your friend Sarah Bennett, Jennifer positively enjoyed being beaten. I have the feeling that further study of the cold and unapproachable Diana might well reap dividends, but that will take time. Now, what else have we?' He looked at the list he had written down. 'Let's go through them one by one. First of all we have Nurse Bennett.' He saw Wainwright's look of resignation. 'All right, George, no more jokes, I promise. Do you think she was telling the truth?'

'It hadn't occurred to me that she wasn't; she's obviously a bit of a gossip, but I wouldn't have thought she was malicious. She clearly didn't like the Matron, Nurse Carter or Miss Fordham much, but she didn't attempt to run any of them down specially.'

'Well, she was lying when she said that she hadn't had an affair with that RMO chap, if what Pritchard said was true, but that in itself may not mean much. She does appear to have been about the only friend that Jennifer had amongst the nurses — everyone seems agreed about that.'

'Pritchard also seems to have been lying, for that matter.'

'Good point; I must say, too, that he seemed to assume that there was something suspicious about Jennifer's death from the moment that I started to discuss it with him, but to be fair, the same could be said about practically everyone to whom we have talked as well. If she really was the love of his life, I suppose he might have been jealous enough to kill her and he would certainly have had the know-how. He's an amoral rogue, but I rather took to him and I don't somehow think that anonymous letters would be his line.'

'Unless of course the murderer and letter writer are two different people.'

'George, the air in this place must be good for you. The other thing that didn't ring true to me was the point about him being in love with her; he mentioned it himself and Miss Banks was very definite about it. Personally, I don't believe it for a moment; not only did he not look like a man who has just lost his true love, but you should have seen the way he was looking at his secretary. It was rather like taking the skin off a banana and a rather ripe one at that. I might say that she loved every minute of it.'

'That theatre sister had a motive all right.'

'Yes, I found her very interesting. Even making allowances for all that gin, she was quite astonishingly frank about herself and equally indiscreet about Pritchard. All that, too, from a woman who almost certainly cheats at golf and under that calm exterior, has a really vicious temper — you should have seen the way she carved up the fairway after missing her approach to the eighteenth green.'

'Why, though, if she had murdered Jennifer, would she have told you all that?'

'Oh, that would be nothing unusual — there's many a murderer who's given him or herself away by having a compulsion to talk about it.'

'What about Miss Fordham?'

'Well, she obviously likes looking at young women with nothing on, but we've no evidence that she takes it further than that and she's generally rather unpopular;

she and Miss Banks are friends and she has the ear of the Matron — nothing all that impressive there, I discovered that they both trained at St Gregory's. She clearly dislikes that RMO chap, but your friend Sarah has explained the reason for that.'

'And then there is Nurse Carter, isn't there, sir?'

Newton gave his assistant a sickly smile. 'All right, George, touché; I'm not saying that you don't deserve a bit of your own back. Well, she brought us the anonymous note in the first place and the only things wrong with her seem to be the old-fashioned virtues of modesty, purity and resource.' Newton threw a piece of toast at Wainwright's head. 'And you can wipe that expression off your face, too.'

The sergeant fielded it neatly. 'I forgot to tell you that Flowerdew, the old porter chap, confirmed her story and the timing.' He glanced across at his superior with what he firmly hoped was an expression of innocence, but which only too obviously a lecherous leer. 'He also said that the girl was obviously very upset about something and he reckoned it was because she wasn't getting her greens.'

'My dear George, that expression went out in the seventeenth century.'

'I dare say it did, but that's what he said.'

'And how, pray, did he arrive at that conclusion.'

'He said he could always tell.' Wainwright took another look at Newton's face and decided to change the subject. 'I still don't see any of that lot actually murdering Jennifer. She seems to have been a funny girl. What do you make of her?'

'I personally have no doubt at all that she had this Huntington's Chorea — it would certainly explain her extraordinarily disturbed sexual behaviour. Thinking of motives, both that man Bradley and his wife for that matter, had ample reason for wanting to get rid of Jennifer and I suppose it's on the cards that she was going in for a spot of blackmail on the side. I can't see either of them, though, having the opportunity of murdering her in that particular way, or any reason why they should want to send anonymous notes. Pritchard, Bradley or that RMO could have been the other half of the 'beast with two backs' and the tenor of the anonymous note raises the possibility that there is a puritanical nut somewhere in the hospital; in many ways, Miss Digby Scott would fit that particular bill best, but that idea's a bit fanciful to say the least.

'From the circumstances in which Jennifer was found, I would have thought that suicide was very unlikely, but I just wonder about something else. I'll have to ask Golding if it's possible, but it did occur to me that she might have died suddenly while getting up to some fun and games and the other person involved had tried to make it look like an accident. That theory might explain the curious position of her legs in the bath.'

'What do we do next?'

'Well, the person I must clearly see next is 'the lascivious Moore'.' Newton got up so quickly that his knee hit the table and a stream of coffee ran across the white table cloth. 'George, I'm a complete idiot. I hadn't heard his name when Pritchard and I were bandying quotations and the connection didn't strike me until a moment ago. It must be him — I have a hunch that if we don't hurry, something very unpleasant may happen to our friend Moore.'

'I'm afraid it has already.'

'What do you mean?'

'Didn't I tell you? Sarah Bennett said he was taken ill a day or so ago and that he was quite bad.'

'George, I don't like the sound of this one little bit — it looks as if Golding was right after all. Come on man, we're going to the hospital.'

Wainwright had to break into a run at intervals to keep up as Newton strode up the road.

'Thanks to you, we're so late that the Secretary should be in by now. There's something curiously literary about this affair, you know George. We have a matron who reads soulful poetry and has a room full of classics and reference books and a surgeon who is hot on his quotations — very odd.'

Wainwright hadn't the slightest idea what he was talking about; indeed he didn't understand a good deal of what Newton said, but at that moment, he wasn't in the least worried; he was still reliving what had happened to him the previous night — to think that he had called Amberstead a one-horse sort of place.

★ ★ ★

Armitage was able to see them almost straight away.

'It's about your RMO, Dr Moore. I hear he's been taken ill and I was wondering if I might see him; normally, of course, I wouldn't want to disturb him, but something rather important has cropped up.'

'I'll see what I can do.' The Hospital Secretary picked up the internal telephone and dialled a number. 'Ah, Stoker, would you please tell me which ward Dr Moore is on? . . . Did you say the intensive care unit? . . . I didn't know he was that bad.' He rang off. 'I must say, this is very worrying. They don't usually transfer people there unless they are very ill indeed. I'll find out if Dr Jenson is available — he's in charge up there and should be able to put you in the picture.'

★ ★ ★

Dr Jenson was a small, dapper little man in his early forties. He shook hands with the two men and motioned them to the chairs in the office by the side of the intensive care unit.

'Well Inspector, what can I do for you?'

'I arrived here a couple of days ago to enquire into the death of one of your student nurses, Jennifer Prentice — the coroner wasn't satisfied about either the cause or the circumstances of it. I discovered something this morning which leads me to believe that Dr Moore's illness might be in some way connected with it. May I ask what's wrong with him?'

'We don't know exactly. He's got some sort of polyneuritis — that's a type of inflammation of the nerves that can lead to paralysis.'

'Is it serious?'

'That depends on the cause.'

'What about in this case?'

'Well, if you want my candid opinion, I don't think he's going to survive.'

'What's the usual cause of polyneuritis?'

'There are a great many, but if it's as acute as this, I suppose one would say it was most likely to be due to some allergic phenomenon or a toxin.'

'Could he have been poisoned?'

Jenson looked up sharply. 'I must say it hadn't occurred to me. The sort of poisons which produce polyneuritis, such as lead and some of the other heavy metals, usually provoke a more chronic illness and Dr Moore was evidently in perfect health until only a week ago. In any case, when one of the staff is taken ill, one doesn't immediately jump to the conclusion that he's been poisoned. Would you like to see him? I should warn you that he's not a very pretty sight.'

There were five beds in the intensive

care unit, but only two were in use. The two men walked across and stood at the foot of the bed on the left. Newton was quite appalled by what he saw. The young man was covered by a single sheet, which came up to his waist. The skin of his face, arms and chest was disfigured by an angry looking rash and continuous involuntary twitching movements were distorting his mouth and eyes. An intravenous infusion was running into one arm and amidst the confusion of pipes, Newton could see that a respirator was pumping air into him by way of a tracheotomy tube. Hardened though he was to unpleasant sights, he could not hide his expression of horror and disgust as he turned away.

'You say he was perfectly well until a week ago; how did his symptoms come on?'

'He had some sort of stomach upset, followed a couple of days later by intensely painful pins and needles in the feet. It was only about forty-eight hours ago that the paralysis started.'

'Look, I wonder if you'd mind if I tell

Golding, the forensic pathologist, about this? He did the autopsy on the nurse and I have a shrewd suspicion that he might be able to throw some light on this.'

'No, of course not.'

'May I use your phone then?'

'Go ahead. I'll be in the lab through that door there, if you want anything else.'

Newton was lucky to find Golding in his office.

'You remember that nurse Jennifer Prentice and your 'brides in the bath' theory?' he said. 'Well, I've been making some enquiries at the hospital and I think someone has been poisoned. If the murderer used a famous model before, it's ten to one that he's done the same thing again. I was wondering if the victim's symptoms would ring any bells with you.'

'What are they?'

'I'm not too *au fait* with all the medical terminology, but I gather he's got a severe polyneuritis which came on after a stomach upset. He's only been ill for a few days, but he looked to me as if he was completely paralysed — he's on a respirator.'

'Anything else?'

'Yes, he's got a rash all over his face and trunk — the skin is scaling badly — and one last thing, he has a lot of funny movements going on around his mouth and eyes.'

'Do they think he's going to recover?'

'No, the doctor here was very gloomy.'

There was a long silence from the other end of the telephone. 'Look here, Newton, I've got an idea.' The detective could hear the other man's excitement. 'Do you think you could get a sample of his urine over here as soon as possible?'

'I'll have to ask the doctor in charge here, of course, but he seems a friendly enough bloke and I don't see why not. I'll bring it up myself this morning if you like. I want to report to Commander Osborne in any case.'

'Capital.'

★ ★ ★

Newton had no difficulty in getting the specimen and as he left the ward he saw Alison Carter in the corridor, looking fresh and cool in her uniform.

'Hello, I didn't expect you to be here.'

'We have to fill in on the wards sometimes when they're short of staff. I'll only have to stay here until midday.'

Newton glanced around; no one was within earshot.

'Look Alison, I think Dr Moore has been poisoned. I want you to keep your eyes and ears open and to let me know if there's any gossip about him, if anyone unexpected has come up here to visit him or if anything unusual at all happens.'

'All right Inspector.'

★　★　★

For the next hour or so, Alison was far too busy and upset to take in fully the implications of what Newton had said. Up to now, in her nursing career, she had not found it too difficult to detach herself emotionally from all the depressing illnesses and situations she had come across, but with someone she knew, even though she didn't like him, it was quite another matter.

157

She had never in her life seen a more distressing sight than the man lying helpless on the bed, made worse by the fact that the last time she had seen him, he had been full of vitality, playing tennis with some of the other doctors on the hospital courts. Even though she didn't understand all the medical details, she was quite experienced enough to realize that his death was inevitable.

When she came off duty, she couldn't face lunch and wandered down towards the town. Ever since Newton had told her of his suspicions about Ian Moore having been poisoned, something had been niggling away in the back of her mind about that wretched quotation, which had been the start of her involvement in the whole business. She knew that she wouldn't be happy until she had had another look at it in the reference book in the public library.

It was one of the Matron's rules that they were not allowed to go into the town in uniform, but Alison couldn't be bothered about that today. She gave a grunt of satisfaction when she saw that the *Oxford Dictionary of Quotations* was on the shelf. She quickly found the page, ran her finger down the column and straight away saw what she was looking for on the line directly below the reference to the 'beast with two backs'.

''The gross clasps of a lascivious Moor.''

Of course, that was it. Although she hadn't known that Ian Moore was going out with Jennifer, she remembered that when she had looked up the quotation before, she had thought it particularly apt. Ian Moore had taken her out to the cinema once and on the way back had asked her in the most explicit and coarse terms if she would let him make love to her. He didn't seem in the least put out when she refused.

'I didn't think you would,' he said with a grin, in fact lascivious was just the adjective she would have applied to it. 'There are plenty of others who will. You don't know what you're missing — I have the reputation of being rather good at it.'

Alison had been shocked by his approach and yet at the same time excited by it. She still hadn't properly made the transition from the cloistered environment of her boarding school, to this atmosphere, where all the prettier student nurses were considered fair game by the young doctors and some who were not so young.

She rather envied the free and easy attitude of girls like Sarah Bennett and knew that she was thought to be prissy and pure. Still, she had the comforting thought that her day would come — perhaps it would be with someone like Roger Newton. She felt a warm glow deep inside her as she thought of him and then blushed scarlet as she saw a middle-aged man looking at her over the top of his book.

Alison walked slowly back to the hospital. It must have been Ian Moore with Jennifer the night she had died and for that matter on the other occasions as well. But why should anyone want to kill them both; it sounded like the work of a lunatic and she gave a little shiver of fright.

Although she hadn't consciously set

out to do so, Alison found herself wandering past the block which contained the residents' quarters. She knew very well which was Ian Moore's window — he was in the habit of leaning out and making remarks when the nurses walked by — and as she went past, she glanced idly in that direction. The curtains were drawn three-quarters of the way across and she looked away again. As she did so, out of the corner of her eye, she could have sworn that she saw a movement. Her gaze snapped back, but it was not repeated and she was almost persuaded that she had imagined the whole thing.

She was well aware that the movement, if there had been one, might have had an innocent explanation — it might have been a draught or even a maid tidying up — but if there was even the slightest chance of finding out anything that would really help Inspector Newton, she was determined to take it.

Alison crept in through the side door, her heart thumping wildly — the residents' quarters were strictly out of bounds to the nurses — and ran up the corridor on tip-toe. She turned the handle and pushed. She had been half hoping that the door would be locked, but it swung open and before her nerve failed her, she went inside.

She let out a gasp of astonishment when her eyes had become accustomed to the darkness. The room was an absolute shambles; books, bed clothes and his personal belongings were strewn all over the floor and even the carpet had been lifted up and thrown on top of the bed. Alison put her head round the door and when she was sure that the coast was clear, fled down the corridor and out into the grounds. Any lingering doubts she had had about Newton's suspicions being correct, had been dispelled completely. She glanced at her watch; it was only half past one and Newton had told her that he wouldn't be back until four-thirty at the earliest. She couldn't think how she was going to get through the afternoon; suppose the murderer had seen her going into Ian Moore's room?

'Nurse Carter!'

Alison stopped dead in her tracks and looked round when she heard the familiar voice.

'I have been looking for you everywhere. Inspector Newton wants to see you urgently at the hotel.'

'But he told me he wouldn't be back until tea time.'

'I know — he discovered something important and decided not to go after all. I tell you what, I'll give you a lift down in my car — it's only just round the corner.'

'Thank you very much.'

Alison got into the car and slammed the door shut.

'Would you mind fastening your seat belt? I feel it's something one should always do, even for the shortest distances.'

When Alison had connected the two pieces of webbing together, the driver gave the free end a strong pull and the belt tightened, the strap digging into her shoulder. Even though it was uncomfortable, Alison felt she couldn't possibly undo it and decided to grin and bear it — after all, the journey would take less than five minutes.

'You won't mind if I deliver a letter on the way, will you? I'm sure that a few minutes won't make any difference.'

Alison only really became suspicious when the car turned into the road that skirted the golf course.

'I thought you said that Inspector Newton wanted to see me urgently.'

She turned sideways and when she saw the expression on the driver's face, tried desperately to release the catch on the safety belt, but a much stronger and larger hand took hers in a grip of iron and at the same time the brakes of the car were slammed on. Alison opened her mouth to scream, but a vicious blow landed on her nose; the tears started to her eyes and before her vision had time to clear, she felt a sharp stab of pain in her right thigh and then a dull gnawing ache in the muscle. She kicked upwards, but only succeeded in hitting her knee an agonizing blow on the fascia and, as if in a dream, saw the syringe with its thick needle being withdrawn.

'I'll teach you to meddle in other people's affairs, you interfering brat.

You'll be seeing your precious Inspector soon enough, but hardly in the place you expected.'

Alison tried to scream, but even to breathe was an effort; the images from her two eyes kept drifting apart and seconds later, she slumped forward unconscious.

8

Golding was peering down his microscope when Newton called in to see him on his way to catch the train from Waterloo back to Amberstead. The pathologist glanced up as his secretary ushered the detective in.

'You were almost certainly correct about that nurse having early Huntington's Chorea. I won't bore you with the details, but there is gliosis of the caudate nucleus and of the corpus striatum as a whole. The changes are slight, but I'm quite convinced that they are significant, particularly in a girl of this age — I'll be able to give you a more definite opinion when the brain has been fixed properly. I must confess that I wouldn't have noticed the abnormalities if you hadn't drawn my attention to the possibility of the disease.'

It was quite obvious to Newton that Golding was in a high state of agitation about something else. His habitual, lugubrious expression was for once absent and if the thought had not been ridiculous, Newton could have sworn that the pathologist was bubbling over with excitement.

The detective smiled. 'You've found out something important in that specimen I brought up, haven't you?'

The pathologist composed himself with some difficulty. 'Yes. I was right, you know, about that murderer of yours,' he said in his usual precise tones, 'no originality, no originality at all.' He shook his head dolefully. 'It was thallium, of course. I have been wondering how long it would be before someone else used it.'

'What made you think of it so quickly?'

'The symptoms you described were absolutely typical.'

'In that case, why didn't they diagnose it at the hospital?'

'Well, you must remember that I had the great advantage of knowing that you yourself suspected that he had been poisoned — not something that most clinicians have in the fore-front of their mind.'

'Wasn't thallium the stuff that Graham Young used in that frightful case a few years ago?'

'Yes, that's right.'

'But I thought it caused the hair to fall out.'

'So it does, but not for two to three weeks and the victim may die long before that if the dose is large enough.'

'What about treatment?'

'Pretty unrewarding, I'm afraid. One can try to remove it from the tissues by using what are called chelating agents, but it doesn't work at all well — I'm afraid that that young man is almost certain to die. I've already taken the liberty of ringing the chap in charge of the case, so that at least they know the correct diagnosis.'

'Is thallium easy to administer?'

'Simplicity itself. It's an odourless substance, which looks rather like ordinary table salt.'

'How difficult would it be for someone to get hold of?'

'Not all that hard, but more so now than it would have been some years ago when it was generally available in most hospitals — it was employed as a depilator in the treatment of ringworm of the scalp.'

'Is it in use for anything else?'

'Yes, quite a few different things — in glass manufacture, as an alloy with tungsten for lamp filaments, in photo-graphic processing, in fireworks and as a rat poison — those are the most important.'

Newton groaned. 'I'll send my assistant round to all the local chemists and so on, but if it's used for as many things as that, I must say it doesn't sound as if he'll have much joy.'

'No, I agree. In my opinion, you'd do much better looking for a psychopath like Graham Young. Find someone like that and you'll have your murderer.'

'I must confess that I'm not getting very far at the moment. Directly I was sure that Moore had been poisoned, though, I spread the word around the hospital just a little; you know what these places are like, it'll be common knowl-edge by now, if I'm any judge. I can only hope that someone will come forward with some useful information.'

'And I can only hope that your murderer doesn't take it into his head to do something even more dramatic,' replied Golding lugubriously. 'If he's copied the methods of two famous killers already, I would suspect that he might try to duplicate a third.'

★ ★ ★

The pathologist's words kept going through Newton's mind as he sat huddled up in a corner seat on the train to Amberstead. If there really was some insane, psychopathic killer in the hospital, the motives for the murders might not be all that obvious. Of all the people he had interviewed, the Matron seemed to be the one with the most on her mind, but that might just be because one of the nurses in her charge had been killed. Now, at least with the thallium, he had a positive clue that they could follow up. He had already telephoned Wainwright from London and the sergeant should have started enquiring at all the local chemists and photographic agents that afternoon.

The train pulled into the station and Newton ignored the expectant taxi drivers, preferring to walk the mile or so back to the hotel. As he strode through the foyer, the receptionist called to him.

'One of the porters brought this note down from the hospital. Said it was most urgent and to give it to you directly you got back.'

'Thanks.'

Newton ripped open the blue envelope and rapidly read the note to himself.

''3.30 p.m. Think I've found the answer in Ian Moore's bedroom. Have gone to the disused range behind the golf course to investigate further. Meet me there as soon as possible. Alison Carter.''

Newton cursed the girl under his breath and then realized that it was mostly his fault. If he hadn't made that remark to her in the intensive care unit, she would never have started to poke her nose into the affair. He was also worried sick about her; if they were dealing with a psychopath and she really had discovered something of importance, then she might be in mortal danger of her life.

But what on earth could the range have to do with it? He took a step towards the reception desk with a view to ringing the hospital, but then changed his mind, deciding that it would achieve nothing and instead scribbled a quick note to Wainwright to tell him where he had gone.

Newton made the five miles to the golf course in about eight minutes. The range was right at the end of the course, just beyond the sixth green and he remembered having seen the access road, which was still used by members of the club if they wanted to start at the seventh tee if the course was busy.

He found the turning without difficulty. The road was both bumpy and sandy and the powerful car snaked from side to side as he accelerated fiercely along it. There was one car parked in the clearing near the seventh tee, but he ignored it and drove past. The road continued for another two hundred yards across the heathland and ahead of him he could see the remains of battered tanks and a concrete wall which was pock-marked with holes made by aircraft cannon shells. There were several concrete block-houses in the distance and a badly weathered notice proclaimed the danger of unexploded shells and warned the public to keep out.'

Eventually the road became obstructed by massive boulders and Newton brought the Rover to a skidding halt, jumped out and looked around. Twenty yards away to his left, he caught sight of a white object and ran across to pick it up. It was a nurse's cap and the name neatly printed on its inner surface, confirmed his worst fears.

'Alison!' he shouted, climbing on a small mound to get a better view.

One by one, he came across her clothes, first one shoe, then the other, her dress, tights, bra and finally her pants. Only a few paces away from the last object was a large, concrete bunker set into the side of a sand hill. The massive steel door was half open.

'Alison?'

He pulled hard on the handle and as the door swung open surprisingly easily, he let out a gasp of horror at the sight in front of him. Alison Carter was facing him, her limbs spread wide, her ankles and wrists being lashed to the wooden shelves, which had obviously at one time been used as racks for shells. Without pausing to think, the detective started forwards.

Newton saw the agonized expression in her eyes and a low moan came from behind the sodden gag in her mouth, but then something hit him a tremendous blow between the shoulders. He stumbled forwards, throwing himself sideways to try to avoid the girl and crashed into the rack. As he struggled to get up, the metal door came to with a loud clang and all the light was shut out.

* * *

The figure outside dropped the heavy section of railway sleeper which had hit the detective and gave a deep sigh of satisfaction. With meticulous care, all the items of clothing were collected and buried in one of the sand hills, all the foot-prints leading to the bunker were smoothed out and the Rover reversed back to the members' car park by the sixth green. It took fifteen minutes for all the wheel tracks to be obliterated and only then did the figure relax, sitting for a moment breathing deeply behind the wheel.

'Not playing today?'

'Oh, hello Colonel Braybrook. No, just been for a walk.'

'You want to avoid that range, you know. Some child was injured by a grenade that went off only last year. Got a new car, I see.'

'No, just borrowed it for the day.'

'Good day to you then.'

'Good day Colonel.'

The man watched while the Rover disappeared down the track, then folded up his trolley, put it and his clubs in the boot of the car and surveyed the scene with quiet pleasure. He had completed the round without one single slice off the tee; it was the monthly medal on the following Thursday and he'd show them this time.

★ ★ ★

'Hang on a jiffy. Let's get some light on the scene shall we?'

Newton snapped on his cigarette lighter, removed the gag and quickly cut through the ropes with his pocket knife.

'You all right?' he asked anxiously.

Alison massaged her wrists and ankles. 'I'm still alive, if that's what you mean.'

Newton marvelled at the girl's courage — her voice was quite steady and when he put the lighter back on again, he could see that she was even managing to raise a smile.

'Attagirl. Now, why not put my jacket on?'

'Thanks, it is a bit damp in here. I'm sorry,' she said when she had sat down with her back to the racks, 'it's all my fault. If I hadn't tried to be clever, all this would never have happened.'

'Tell me about it,' he said gently.

When he had sat down beside her and taken her hand in his, she described her visit to the Public Library, how she came to look at Ian Moore's room and the way she had been tricked into getting into the car.

'When I recovered consciousness I was tied up in here. She's sick that woman, you know Roger.' He felt her shiver slightly. 'She told me all the things she would have liked to do to me if she had had enough time — I was only saved from it because it took me much longer to come round than she had planned.'

'I suppose she must have seen you go into Moore's room and assumed you knew more than you did. Did she force you to write that note?'

'What note?'

Newton let out an audible groan. 'You'd never think that I'd been doing this job for ten years, would you? There was a letter waiting for me at the hotel when I got back — I've got it in my pocket here. It never occurred to me that you hadn't written it — as far as I was aware, you and George Wainwright were the only people who knew that I'd gone to London and wouldn't be back until tea time. That's how I was lured out here, of course, the note said that you had found a clue in Moore's bedroom and were going out to the range to investigate.'

'Does anyone know that you're here?'

'I left a note for Wainwright. He'll be out here before long and when he finds the car, he'll soon have us out.'

'Supposing she's moved it?'

'I'm sure he'll come just the same. In any case, it'll do no harm to see if we can get out ourselves.'

Newton was in fact the very reverse of sure that Wainwright would be able to find them. If their assailant had had the skill to trap them both like this, it was highly unlikely that she wouldn't have taken care to avoid leaving any clues as to their whereabouts within the precincts of the range. Even if he did come and started to search, he wouldn't know where to start and it would need a platoon of men to do the job properly and night would have fallen long before that could be organized.

There was clearly no profit in dwelling on it or thinking about what he should have done, so he set out to explore the bunker. It was a good deal longer than Newton had realized, being some twenty feet in length and roughly twelve feet wide. The wooden racks, which were rotten with age, were arranged in four rows running the whole length of the building and there was a narrow passage between each of them. The floor was covered with an inch or two of sand, but when he probed it with his pocket knife, he could feel the concrete underneath.

The door was made of solid steel and he remembered having seen that it was secured on the outside by a metal bar. He ran his finger all the way round the edge and looked at it both with his lighter and in the dark. To his dismay, he saw that there was no chink of light showing round the edge, not the merest breath of air coming in and there was no key hole.

Even though the door had only been shut for a few minutes, the atmosphere was already beginning to feel stuffy. He had no accurate idea how long the air inside would last the two of them, but at best it could only be a matter of a few hours.

'Can I do anything to help?'

'Before long we're going to run short of oxygen and I'm going to have a go at the concrete with my penknife. If I can only make some sort of hole through to the outside, we should be all right. You can help most for the time being by lying still and breathing as quietly as possible.'

Long before he gave up, Newton realized that the task was hopeless; at its thinnest, the concrete must have been several inches thick and his pocket knife was only a flimsy affair. When he snapped off the smaller of the two blades, he had hardly made any impression at all.

'I'm afraid that that idea was a non-starter,' he said. 'I'm going to have a look round the rest of the place before the lighter packs up.'

A careful examination of the walls revealed nothing useful and when he had finished, he glanced up at the ceiling.

'I say, Alison, would you hold the

lighter up here for a moment, I've got an idea.'

He climbed on top of one of the wooden racks and began to inspect the electric light assembly.

'What is it?'

'Well, you can see that the wires to the socket here where the bulb used to be are carried in this metal conduit. If I can detach it and pull the wires through, it might just possibly let some air in.'

The metal conduit was rusty and once he had prised it free from one of the clips attaching it to the ceiling, he was able to get some leverage and break it away from the metal grille which had at one time protected the bulb. The wires were then exposed and he was able to cut through them without difficulty.

'Wish me luck.'

He wound the wires round his finger and gave them a sharp tug. There was a momentary resistance, then suddenly he felt something give and he was able to pull them through. When the wires had come away completely, he put his cheek against the end of the metal conduit and after a few moments shook his head dolefully.

'No good?'

' 'Fraid not.'

'It was a jolly good try anyhow.'

He clambered down, beginning to feel the hopelessness of the situation eating into his morale.

'There's only one thing left.'

'What's that?'

'The floor. I'm very much afraid that it's likely to be solid concrete like the walls and if that's the case, we've had it, but where there's hope . . . '

Almost the whole of the floor was covered with a thin layer of sand and he began to sound it systematically with the longer blade of his penknife, covering the area from side to side in parallel lines, roughly two feet apart. He was on his fourth traverse when the blade of the knife made an entirely different sound and he distinctly felt it bite into some much softer material.

'Alison! I think I'm on to something; it feels like wood under here.' He quickly mapped its extent with the knife. 'It's about two feet square — could be a trap door.'

Newton scraped all the sand away and when he snapped his lighter on, saw that he had been correct.

'Where do you think it leads to?'

'I can't imagine, but there's only one way to find out.'

The detective freed the iron ring and pulled up hard. Initially the cover failed to shift, but after he had jumped on it a few times and removed some of the sand from the crack between it and the concrete surround, he felt it give a fraction of an inch and moments later, he was able to open it fully.

'Well, that's the anti-climax of the century,' he said, panting hard after his exertions. The hole in the floor was completely filled with sand. 'There must be some explanation for it; nobody in their senses would build a trapdoor into the floor of a place like this unless it had a purpose.'

'Did they ever build these things on stilts?' said Alison after a long pause.

'I don't know, I'm afraid, but I don't

see why they would want to go to all that trouble. What had you in mind?'

'I was just thinking that they must have been built at least thirty years ago and in that time, the sand could easily have shifted and piled up underneath. Suppose they had built it into the side of a sand hill and had stilts in front to prevent it from subsiding. They might have wanted the entrance elevated so that it was on a level with the tail-boards of lorries and the trapdoor might have been another point of access.' She misinterpreted his silence. 'Perhaps it wasn't such a good idea after all.'

'Don't get me wrong, it's a most ingenious theory — I only wish I'd thought of it myself. I was just trying to work out its implications. Hang on a second, I'm going to try a little experiment.'

He plunged his hand into the soft sand and began to feel this way and that.

'What are you doing?'

'Just seeing if the trapdoor leads to a shaft or whether there is any possibility of digging a tunnel to the outside.'

'What's the verdict?' she asked a few minutes later.

'Well, the concrete's about four inches thick and I've been able to get my hand under it without any difficulty.'

'Do you think you might be able to bore a tunnel?'

'I have no doubt of it, unless of course the sand is terribly dry and soft, which it doesn't feel like, and the further down I went, the more damp it felt.'

'But wouldn't there be a terrible risk of a tunnel collapsing even if the sand is good? My efforts at the sea-side always seem to end like that.'

'Mine do too, but that's usually because the roof caves in. Here, with the concrete above, we won't have that trouble and if we shore up the side walls with some of the wood here, I reckon it would be pretty safe.'

'Shall we have a go then? We've got nothing to lose.'

'I'm afraid that's not strictly true — you know that I said earlier that we'd be running short of oxygen.'

'Yes.'

'Heavy work, such as tunnelling is bound to be, would increase the oxygen consumption enormously. I don't know by how much, of course, but I would guess that it would double or treble it, which would cut down the time we can live in here by a corresponding amount. There's one other thing, too.'

'What's that?'

'We're assuming that your theory is correct. It may prove quite impossible to get out that way.'

'I see. So it's a question of tunnelling successfully on the one hand and hoping that someone will rescue us on the other.'

'Exactly. Any views yourself?'

' "Better to travel hopefully . . . " '

Newton chuckled. 'I know what you mean, but I'm afraid that the quotation isn't all that apt.'

'How should it really go?'

' "To travel hopefully is a better thing than to arrive, and the true success is to labour." It's Robert Louis Stevenson.'

'I've got myself into enough trouble with quotations already, perhaps I'd do better to give up trying.'

'Never say die. I agree with you anyway; I think we should have a go.'

'What would you like me to do?'

'While I start on the digging — I thought I'd use one of my shoes — perhaps you could break off some strips of wood about two feet long. Later on, when I make some headway under the floor, I'll use both shoes and you can reach down and empty them — it'll be a sort of conveyor belt system.'

At the beginning, Newton made rapid progress and within half an hour had made a start on the horizontal section beneath the concrete floor. The sand was on the soft side, which made the digging easy, but he was very glad of the strips of wood, which prevented the side walls from caving in. Although he knew that the possibility was a largely theoretical one, he was nevertheless terrified that the tunnel would collapse on him and that he would be buried alive.

The sand was everywhere, in his hair, in his eyes and in his ears — he could even feel it gritting between his teeth. Although time and again he nearly gave up, he kept forcing himself to do one more shoeful and so he continued.

With every passing minute, his breathing was becoming more laboured and finally he lay utterly exhausted. He operated the catch on his lighter to check on the time, but although the flame caught, within seconds it began to flicker and then went out. Even before he had checked to make sure that it was not the gas which had run out, he knew perfectly well that their oxygen was almost exhausted.

Newton forced himself to think calmly and calculated that he must be within eighteen inches of the front wall of the bunker. He began to make a hole in the face of the tunnel with his right hand, but had only buried his arm up to the elbow when his index finger hit something hard and a spasm of pure horror set his heart hammering in his chest as he realized the full hopelessness of the situation.

He poked around for a bit longer with his pocket knife, but it was only too obvious that his way was totally obstructed. Slowly and painfully he edged himself backwards out of the tunnel and as he emerged, he could hear the rasping quality of Alison's breathing.

'What's up?' she said hoarsely.

'It's no good, I'm afraid. I hit solid concrete; the trapdoor must just have led to another underground store.'

Alison put her arms round his neck. 'What a shame after all that work — it was a marvellous effort.'

Newton dragged himself across the floor and sat with his back against the wall, while she lay on the sandy floor with her head on his lap.

'We're not going to get out of this, are we?'

It wasn't really a question, she was just calmly stating a fact.

'Things don't look too rosy, I must confess; we'll just have to hope that George does his stuff.'

'I don't want to die, Roger. It's not so much that I'm afraid, but there are so many things I haven't done.' He ran his fingers gently through her hair. 'Are you married, Roger?'

'No, I haven't found anyone yet foolish enough to be prepared to put up with me. Anyway, it's no sort of a life being married to a C.I.D. man.'

'Tell me what you do?'

Although talking was a great effort, it made the situation easier to bear. He told her all about his job, the interesting times as well as the boring, the exciting and the tedious, the humorous and the macabre. For her part, she told him about her family, her schooling and her hopes for the future.

'You know,' she said after they had been silent for some time, 'I would never have thought that I could have discussed this with anyone, but there have been times when I have envied Sarah Bennett and even Jennifer, enormously.'

'What! You must be joking.'

'No, I mean it. You may not believe it, nurses' reputations being what they are, but I'm ... I'm ... I mean I've never ... '

Newton stroked her cheek. 'I believe you.'

'That's really my trouble,' she said with

a sigh. 'Everyone believes it, that's why they never try, and it's not that I don't want to — I do desperately at times. You can't imagine what I've felt like at times, hearing what's been going on in Jennifer's bedroom. You don't think there's anything wrong with me do you?'

'You're the most attractive girl I've ever met. The only trouble with you is that you've come to believe all that you read and hear in the media. The ones you should be feeling sorry for are the promiscuous ones like your friend Sarah. You may think that she's having a good time now, but consider what she'll be like when she's thirty-five and running to fat. Sleeping around can almost become an addiction.'

'What's it really like?' There was a long pause and Alison felt his finger, which had been tracing intricate patterns around her ear, suddenly become motionless. 'You didn't mind me asking, did you?'

'I feel flattered that you should have — I was just trying to think up an honest reply. Your question is of course in a sense impossible to answer. It can be the greatest experience possible or one of the most disappointing; it all depends on the circumstances and the people involved. For some, it only works in marriage, for others at other times as well. When the right time and the right person comes along, it will work all right for you — I know it will.'

'But how will I know who the right person is?'

'You'll know.'

'I think I do.'

He gave a little chuckle.

'What's so funny?'

'It's just that I bet I know what you're doing now.'

'What's that?'

'Blushing.'

Alison laughed. 'No, I'm not; that's one of the reasons why I'm so sure. If we get out of this alive, will you show me?'

'If you still want me to then.'

'Don't worry, I will.'

For some time, they had been having to pause between sentences and they were both beginning to feel light-headed and unreal. Newton had to bend forward to catch her whisper.

'It won't be long now, will it?'

He kissed her gently. 'See if you can get off to sleep.'

Within a few minutes, she seemed to have lapsed into unconsciousness. Slowly, taking care not to disturb her, he pulled an old envelope out of the pocket of his jacket, which she was still wearing and wrote a few lines on it with his pencil in the dark — even if they weren't found in time, he was determined that that mad-woman wouldn't get away with it. When he had finished, he stroked her cheek gently with his finger and then he, too, closed his eyes.

9

Miss Digby Scott heard about Newton's suspicions when she went to the intensive care unit as part of her morning round and all the colour drained out of her face; this was too much of a coincidence and she was going to have to do something about it now, whatever it cost.

'Are you feeling all right, Miss Digby Scott?'

The Assistant Matron, who was accompanying her on the round, looked at her anxiously.

'No, I've not been feeling myself all morning. I'll have to ask you to take over, I'm afraid.'

'Let me take you back to your flat. I'll call the acting RMO.'

'No thank you, it's nothing — just a migraine coming on, that's all. I'll go and lie down for a spell.'

When she got back to her flat, Diana Digby Scott took the familiar newspaper cutting out of a drawer in her desk. It had become discoloured with age and she knew the contents by heart, but she read every word of it again, her fingers, as they held it, trembling uncontrollably. When she had finished, she sat for a few minutes staring out of the window and then with sudden decision, picked up the phone.

'Give me an outside line, would you please?'

She made two calls, changed quickly out of her uniform and having made sure that the newspaper cutting was in her handbag, hurried down the stairs.

The Assistant Matron would have been astonished to have seen Miss Digby Scott leaving the hospital grounds by a side entrance and even more so to have seen her running to catch the bus to the station. She would even have said that such an event was an impossibility; whatever the situation, however grave the crisis, the Matron never ran. Diana Digby Scott had even surprised herself; now that the decision had been taken, she felt a new sense of purpose.

She spent an exhausting day in London

and on the way back, sat in the train trying to control the almost ungovernable rage that had been threatening to break loose ever since she had discovered the truth. To think that she had put up with four years of utter misery, misery such that she had even contemplated suicide, all for nothing. How could she have been so stupid as not to have checked on it before? But of course at the time it had seemed all so utterly clear and damning. One thing was certain and that was that she was going to put a stop to it and what was more, that very night.

Directly she got back to her flat, she rang the intensive care unit.

'This is the Matron here. Would you please tell me how Dr Moore is getting on? . . . What? When did it happen? . . . I see. Have his relatives been informed? . . . I'm so glad that they arrived in time.'

She sat for a moment, tense and drawn, then reached for the phone and was put through to the hotel. It was a good five minutes before the operator was able to locate Sergeant Wainwright.

'You say he went out several hours ago?

When will he be back?'

'I'm afraid I've no means of knowing. Is it urgent? Is there anything I can do to help?'

Diana Digby Scott hesitated. Although she had not even spoken to the Sergeant before, she had the feeling that he was not the right man to deal with a situation like this.

'Would you please ask him to ring me as soon as he gets back? It is a matter of the very greatest importance.'

She managed to wait another hour, but then could stand it no longer; there were some questions that she needed to have answered and there was only one person who could do it. If she had stopped to consider the matter, she would probably have realized that she was running herself into personal danger, but she was past coherent thought.

She pressed the buzzer on her desk and a few minutes later, the maid sidled into the room.

'Winnie, I want you to find Miss Fordham and tell her to come here now. I don't care where she is or what she is doing; I want her to come here now. Tell her I have some important news for her concerning Dr Moore.' The old woman turned to go. 'And Winnie, when she gets here, on no account am I to be disturbed. Is that absolutely clear?'

When the maid had gone, she sat bolt upright in her chair behind the desk with her eyes shut, those all too familiar events going remorselessly through her mind.

★　★　★

Life for Diana Digby Scott had for many years been a series of predictable and highly successful steps, until that summer evening nine years earlier.

The daughter of upper middle class parents — her father was still a County Court Judge — she went to a famous girls' boarding school near to her home in Bath. Her stay there was an unqualified success. Above average at her work, good at games, personable and well connected, almost inevitably she became head girl. In due course, she got an upper second in English at university and when she took up nursing, it was assumed that one day she would become the matron of one of the famous London teaching hospitals.

Three years older than the rest of her set, while not exactly unpopular, she never fitted in well with the rest of them. As one of the others put it, Diana was just too well off, too well connected, too elegant, too well behaved — in fact too good to be true.

The two people whom Diana Digby Scott couldn't stand were June Fordham and her friend Grace Ryan. A great one for practical jokes, June also had a coarse sense of humour, never more in evidence than when the refined Diana was about and she used to take an absolute delight in trying to embarrass her at every possible opportunity. Diana, for her part, treated her with icy politeness tinged with contempt, something that made the other girl long to crack the façade of effortless superiority.

June Fordham's opportunity came at the party after their final exams. Inevitably, Diana had won the gold medal and June had not found it difficult to recruit three others who were equally jealous of her success, to help her.

June had come up to her while she was standing on her own in a corner, sipping a gin and tonic.

'I say Diana, would you mind coming to have a look at Patricia? She's been taken ill — a couple of the others are with her in the bathroom.'

Diana went along with her, quite unsuspecting, and only realized that something was up when June slipped the bolt across the door behind her and she saw the three grinning girls facing her.

'What do you think you're up to?' She did her best to appear calm, but inside her she could feel the fear beginning to build up.

'You've had this coming to you for a long time, Miss High and Mighty — you think you're so grand with that university degree we never stop hearing about. Do you know what we're going to do? We're going to strip you mother naked and dump you into a bath of cold water. What would Daddy have to say about that?'

Diana licked her lips. Despite all her

years at boarding school, she was still shy about her body and hated to be seen undressed.

'You wouldn't dare.'

'Wouldn't we just. Come on girls.'

Diana fought like a mad thing, but she was no match for the four of them and before long, the last of her clothes had been ripped off and she lay spreadeagled, face down on the lino, each girl holding on to one of her limbs.

'Please let me go, you've had your fun.'

Grace Ryan gripped Diana's hair with her free hand and pulled her head back off the ground.

'We've hardly started yet, have we June?'

The other girl looked up, grinning widely. 'No, indeed not. Fill up the bath, Grace.'

The red-haired girl who had been holding Diana's right arm, got up and went across to the taps.

'How about warming her up a bit, June?' she said. 'This water's freezing.'

'Good idea.'

June Fordham reached across and

201

picked up the long handled bath brush.

Diana's eyes opened wide with terror as she saw what the other girl was going to do. 'If you don't let me go, someone's going to get hurt,' she said between sobs, tears of misery and humiliation streaming down her cheeks.

'You're so right and who do you think it's going to be?'

She lifted the brush high up in the air and Diana let out a high pitched scream.

'Go easy June. Don't you think she's had enough?'

'Don't be so soft Connie. I haven't even started yet.'

She had just started to bring the brush down, when there was a sharp crack and almost simultaneously, the girl who had been kneeling on Diana's shoulder, let out a high pitched yell of pure agony.

'She's broken my finger,' she screamed.

'Let me go or I'll start on the next one.'

'No — o — o. June, for God's sake let her go.'

Diana started to bend the next finger back and the girl began to scream again. June slowly released her leg and Diana got to her feet and, still maintaining her grip, dragged the other girl up with her.

'Now get out — all of you.'

'It was only a bit of fun — you had no right to hurt Connie like that.'

'If that's your idea of fun June, it's not mine. I'm warning you, try anything like that again and I'll kill you.'

June, who had been thinking of getting Connie away and finishing the job properly, shrank back as she saw the expression on Diana's face. At that moment, she really believed the threat. The others filed out, Connie holding her injured hand and moaning softly.

June was the last one to leave. 'One of these days, Miss Diana Digby-bloody-Scott, one of these days,' she muttered to herself as she slammed the door behind her.

*   *   *

Much to Diana's relief, June Fordham left the hospital soon after; there was some sort of row, but she never discovered exactly what the trouble was.

Her own career continued smoothly on the lines that everyone had predicted. Despite her late start, she became one of the youngest sisters ever to be appointed to her teaching hospital and then, at the age of thirty-two, she became Matron at St Aldhelm's.

She had been there about two years when she received the invitation to Constance Blakelock's wedding. Seeing her name again after all those years brought back all the memories of the incident in the bathroom and her first impulse had been to refuse. The more she thought about it though in the next few days, the more did she realize that she needed a break and it would be nice to see some of her old set again. She had been working too hard and it would do her good to go out for a change.

If Constance wanted to bury the hatchet, so well and good. She had always regretted having hurt her so badly when it had been perfectly obvious right from the start that it had been June who had been the ring-leader.

The wedding was held at eleven o'clock

and Diana drove down from the hospital that morning. She was a few minutes late and slipped into the back of the church just as the service was beginning. She was a bit shaken to see that two of the girls who had attacked her in the bathroom were bridesmaids and several rows in front of her she caught sight of both June and Grace, who were sitting together. At the reception, though, not only did she meet several old friends, but all four of them were obviously determined to be agreeable and any reservations she had had about the wisdom of coming, were soon dispelled.

As she shook hands with Constance and kissed her on the cheek, she couldn't help glancing down at the girl's left hand and noticing the slight thickening of her index finger.

'Diana! How lovely to see you; your present was really beautiful. I don't think you've met David.'

The moment had passed and after a glass or two of champagne, Diana began to relax. She felt her heart beating a little faster when June Fordham came up to her, but she need not have worried; the other woman was obviously on her best behaviour and determined to be as pleasant as possible.

'Congratulations on your job,' she said. 'I meant to write, but you know how it is. Anyhow, better late than never.'

'Thanks very much. It was a bit of a struggle to start with — you know what it's like taking over from someone who's been in a place for ages, but it's beginning to get a bit easier now. How about you? What have you been up to?'

'Oh, I've been knocking about the place a bit. I did some private nursing abroad for a time and I'm looking after an old woman in London at the moment. The job's a bit of a drag, but she's got pots of money and I must say the pay's very good.'

Despite her obvious good intentions, a little of June Fordham went a very long way, but she stuck to Diana like a leech and there was no escaping her even at lunch. Their place names had been put next to each other, but at least there was someone else she knew sitting on the other side of the table.

It was in the middle of the afternoon, just before she was thinking of starting to drive back, that Diana began to feel ill. It was true that she had had a fair amount to drink, but not enough to make her so heavy headed and dizzy, and she couldn't believe it was that. She felt unreal and the voices of the people around her lost their clarity.

'I say Diana, you look a bit rough. Would you like me to come back with you? I can get a train back from Amberstead.'

'Would you June? I wonder if you'd mind driving, I feel a bit giddy?'

'I'm not much good I'm afraid; I do have a licence, but I've had no practice for years. I tell you what, if you drive out of the town, I'll carry on from there.'

'All right then.'

★ ★ ★

Diana Digby Scott remembered almost nothing of that journey. She recalled setting out and although she realized vaguely that she was unfit to drive, in some strange way her will seemed to have become totally sapped. There was an agonized shout in her ear, the appalling pain in her face and then nothing.

When she recovered consciousness, her face felt stiff and she had great difficulty in breathing through her nose. She looked through her swollen eye-lids and gradually took in the fact that she was in her own bed. She tried to sit up, but a restraining hand pushed her back. As her vision came back into focus, she saw June Fordham looking down at her.

'June! What are you doing here?'

'You had an accident.'

'What sort of accident?'

'Look Diana, I'm afraid that things are rather serious. You had too much to drink at the wedding and you were driving rather wildly on the way back here. I tried to make you stop, but you wouldn't and then it happened.' June looked away from her.

'What happened, for God's sake?'

'You hit someone.'

'Were they badly hurt?'

'It was a child, a girl of about six, and you killed her, Diana.'

The woman lying on the bed went ashen white and collapsed back against the pillows. 'No,' she said in a harsh whisper, 'it's not possible. Did you call the police?'

'No. The child was dead; there was nothing to be done, so I drove the car back here.'

'But you couldn't have left a child lying there dead by the side of the road.'

'That's a lot of thanks, I must say. Do you realize what would have happened if the police had come? You would never have passed the breathalyzer test; you would have been up for manslaughter and you would have gone to prison for an absolute cert. Nothing I could have done would have brought the child back to life and I couldn't bear the thought of your career being in ruins.'

In the months to come, Diana Digby Scott liked to think that if she had been in a more normal frame of mind, she would have gone to the police herself. It was true that she had felt unwell at the wedding and she knew that she should never have set out on the journey, but she couldn't believe that she had been drunk.

For the fortnight following her return to consciousness, she spent most of her time in bed, with June ministering to her every need. During the whole of this time, she seemed incapable of making any decisions; she slept for hours at a time and when she did wake up, felt heavy headed and dopey. June had made up some tale about her having had a fall and her long period of convalescence was put down to concussion.

When eventually she did get back to work and June had gone, she very nearly did take the decision to report the matter to the police, but apart from the fact that it would certainly get June into serious trouble as well, it was the thought of what it would do to her father that finally dissuaded her. She went through agonies of self recrimination and even had the idea that the whole business might have been one of June's more macabre practical jokes, but she realized that this was just wishful thinking, particularly when she remembered how badly her face had been injured and when she inspected her car.

The glass in the near-side headlight was broken, there was a large dent in the wing and the ultimate horror was the small dark patch near the outside mirror. She desperately wanted to believe that it wasn't blood, but she scraped a little off and the pathology department confirmed her worst fears. They were even able to tell her the group.

Diana Digby Scott tried to forget the whole affair and threw herself into her work even harder than ever. She sold her car and, inconvenient though it was, decided never to drive again. She had to do something by way of atonement and this gesture, small though it was, was better than nothing. Little did she realize at the time that her punishment was only just beginning.

Some six months after the incident, the Sister Tutor left to become Assistant Matron at another hospital and the post was advertised in the nursing press. Within a week, a letter arrived from June

Fordham. Its meaning was only too clear; she was applying for the job and what was more, she expected to get it. There were no actual threats in her letter, but there could be no misinterpreting the newspaper cutting with its terrible headline: 'HIT AND RUN DRIVER KILLS FARMER'S DAUGHTER.'

Diana Digby Scott had to work hard to get June Fordham the job. The woman had no worthwhile references, no background of teaching and did not impress at the interview. To make matters even more difficult, there was an outstanding candidate from one of the London teaching hospitals. She got her way in the end, but only by digging in her toes and refusing to agree to the other girl's appointment. If one of the lay members of the committee had not wanted her support on some other matter, she was sure that she would never have achieved it.

June was not as utterly disastrous in the job as Diana had expected. In the administrative sense, she was quite efficient and did not try to throw her weight about too much. Soon, however, the Matron began to hear rumours about her behaviour, rumours of a nature similar to those that had also been circulating in their days together at St Gregory's. Finally, Diana had no choice other than to tackle her about them.

'Look here June,' she said one day, 'I have had complaints from the RMO about the way you handle the medical examinations for the first year nurses.'

'Oh! And what has Dr Moore to say about me?'

'He says it is quite unnecessary to have them waiting stark naked before he sees them and I agree with him. It is both humiliating and embarrassing for them and it has got to stop.'

'You're hardly in a position to dictate to me, you know Diana.'

'Don't press me too hard, June; have you forgotten what happened when you did once before. And another thing, there have been rumours about you and Jennifer Prentice; I don't want to know whether they are true or not, but if I hear any more of them, you'll be dismissed, even if it means ruin for me. Now get out, before I lose my temper.'

★ ★ ★

Diana Digby Scott was shaken out of her reverie by the sound of the door opening at the base of the stairs. Her eyes snapped open, but otherwise she didn't move.

'Come in June, sit down. All right, thank you Winnie, that will be all.' She waited until the door was shut and then thrust the newspaper cutting across the desk. 'I went up to London today June and saw my uncle — he's the music critic on one of the Sunday papers. I must say they were most obliging up there; it took them several hours, but they were able to trace it in the end. It came from one of the Yorkshire evening papers — that's quite a long way from Dorset, isn't it June? And what about the date? A good six weeks before the wedding, wasn't it? You had it all planned hadn't you? There never was an accident, was there? You drugged me at the reception, waited until I was almost unconscious, then shouted

214

and hit me in the face.'

'Actually I pushed you forward on to the steering wheel and a great deal of pleasure it gave me too. Don't forget the bashed in wing and the dried blood. I thought they were rather nice touches.'

'You're mad.'

'On the contrary, it's you who ought to have had your brains examined. Do you think I would have been taken in by something like that, clever though it was? The trouble with you Diana, is that you are fettered by moral scruples. It never occurred to you that I could have done anything like that, now did it? I needed the job here and the getting of it required a great deal of thought and planning and also gave me the opportunity of taking you down a peg or two, something you richly deserved. Of course I took a lot of risks, but that was half the fun of it; you wouldn't understand, you're not a gambler by nature, are you? I made a bet with myself that you wouldn't check that newspaper cutting at the time or go to the police and I was right, wasn't I? What made you think of doing so today?'

'After what had happened to Jennifer Prentice, when I heard about Dr Moore, I just knew.'

'You must be getting psychic in your old age, my dear Diana, but it's a bit late in the day, isn't it?'

'For four years, you've led me to believe that I killed a child.'

'Do you know what I'd have done in your place when I found out? I'd have killed the person responsible and have thought up some suitable and subtle way of doing it.'

'I really believe you would, particularly after my visit to St Gregory's today. The matron took a bit of persuading, but I finally found out why you left so suddenly.'

'They had their suspicions, but they never proved it, you know. They could have done, but the thought of all the scandal was too much for them. Anyhow, it wasn't as if I'd even killed her, but I must say she wasn't up to much by the time I had finished with her. Did they tell you who it was? . . . No, I didn't think they would. It was that sister tutor, you know. Yes, that's right, the one who was always getting at me and holding you up as a shining example. She used to make me sick, but I made her a good deal sicker.' She let out a high pitched giggle. 'Arsenic it was.'

'Why did you kill Jennifer Prentice and Dr Moore?'

'Nobody treats me like he did and gets away with it. He threatened to speak to his uncle and have me dismissed; I believe he would have done too.'

'But why Jennifer Prentice?'

'She and I were getting along very nicely until that bastard came along, then he found out about it and stopped her from seeing me. She should never have let herself be influenced by him and I had to punish her for that. It'll take me years to find another like her.'

'What do you mean?'

'Well, you no doubt remember, my dear Diana, that I rather like hitting people — I always have regretted that I wasn't able to finish the job that evening in the bathroom.' Miss Digby Scott flushed at the memory of it. 'I caught

Jennifer climbing in early one morning and half in fun, I gave her the choice of being reported to you and probably being thrown out, or receiving an appropriate punishment from me. 'What would you suggest?' she said, giving me a funny look.' A dreamy expression came over June Fordham's face. 'Do you know, she liked receiving it every bit as much as I enjoyed giving it to her. That first time, I made her take all her clothes off and hit her as hard as I could with my riding crop. She never made a sound, even though it must have hurt like the very devil; I made up for it after, though.'

'You can spare me the sordid details. Why did you send that anonymous letter?'

'To make them both suffer a bit, that's why. I sent several in fact and even took a quotation from that book of yours over there and typed the envelopes on your machine.' She giggled again. 'I also remembered to do it with two fingers so that they would think that it had been done by a novice; naturally I let Newton know that I had had a secretarial training.

It wouldn't surprise me if that policeman hadn't been on the point of arresting you, although it's a bit late in the day now.

'I must admit that I had a bit of luck with Ian Moore, but they say that fortune favours the brave, don't they? He wasn't as much of a fool as he looked — he knew I'd sent those notes. I thought I'd better search his room just before he died and I found a letter addressed to his uncle, which he hadn't had time to post before he was taken ill. Not mind you that it would have made all that much difference in the long run, but it would have made things more difficult for me. I left one of your handkerchiefs in his room too; even those stupid flatfoots should get that message.'

Miss Digby Scott reached out an arm for the telephone. 'You are mad, June, and you are going to be put out of harm's way. The Inspector will be back by now.'

'Really Diana, you're rather pathetic, you know. Do you think I would be sitting here chatting if I hadn't already dealt with that stupid policeman?' She looked at her watch. 'I should think that they will have run out of air by now.'

'What are you talking about?' Miss Digby Scott had turned ashen white.

'I locked him and the pure Nurse Carter up safely somewhere; they're probably both dead by now.' She giggled once more. 'She's not bad when one gets her clothes off, not bad at all.'

'You'll never get away with it; I'll ring the Sergeant.'

'You're not going to ring anyone, now or ever again. I heard you tell Winnie that you didn't want to be disturbed — very convenient I must say. Do you know what I'm going to do Diana?' She opened her handbag and took out a syringe full of a faintly yellow liquid. 'I'm going to inject you with this pentothal — I don't need to tell you how quickly it works — and when you're unconscious, I'm going to put you in the bath and cut your wrists with a razor blade. You should be nice and floppy and there should be no difficulty about making it look like suicide and I doubt if they'll think of checking your blood barbiturate level. Most of it will have gone into the bath water in any case.' She laughed mirthlessly. 'Rather a neat idea, isn't it? What will Daddy think of that? I've made a study of this sort of thing for years, you know; I wouldn't be surprised if I get into the textbooks myself one day.'

Diana Digby Scott's mouth was so dry that her voice was barely audible. She leaned across the desk.

'When the Matron of St Gregory's hears what has happened, she'll know you were responsible. They'll catch you, they're bound to.'

'Oh no they won't. Do you really think I hadn't planned for this sort of eventuality? You knew that I'd done some private nursing, didn't you? Well, that last old lady was ever so devoted to me — left me quite a lot in her will as a matter of fact.'

'I suppose you killed her too.'

'Just helped her along the way a little. I hadn't really intended to leave this country — the set-up here suited me quite admirably — but it looks as if I shall have to, much as I would have liked to be around to see if my little plan for you works. I'll just have to make do with reading about it in the papers — I can't see it being kept out of the National Dailies. I doubt if they'll ever find our two love birds — did you see them making eyes at each other — I might even drop the law a line about it. I'd certainly have sent you a post-card, but then of course you won't be here to receive it. Well, much as I have enjoyed our little chat, the time has come I think, don't you?'

She held the syringe up to the light and expelled the last bit of air. She was lowering it again, when she saw the movement across the desk. She just had time to raise her hand, when something hit her a terrible blow on the forehead and she fell back unconscious.

Diana Digby Scott wiped the sweat from her brow and picked up the heavy glass paperweight from the floor. June must have been half blinded when she looked up at the light; she had never seen it coming. The Matron went down on one knee and leaned over the unconscious woman. There was a large swelling coming up on her forehead, but she was breathing easily and her pulse was quite regular.

June Fordham was no light-weight and it took her ten minutes to lift her back into the seat and bind her safely. The chair was a heavy one and Miss Digby Scott secured her wrists and ankles to its arms and legs with several turns of broad sticky tape. When she had finished, she poured herself a stiff drink and settled down to wait.

It was not long before the Sister Tutor began to stir, but she forced herself to wait until the woman's eyes opened and she seemed to be fully conscious, then stood up in front of her.

'June, tell me what you have done with the Inspector and Nurse Carter.'

She could see the fury in the other woman's eyes as she shook her head violently.

'Only if you let me go.'

'I wouldn't let you go, not even to save my life. Tell me where they are.'

'Go to hell.'

'I'm not a violent person by nature,

June, but I'm not going to let those two die. Don't push me too far; you saw once before what I am capable of doing. I'll ask you one final time. Where are they?'

The only reply was a stream of obscenities.

'Very well, if you don't tell me, I shall start breaking your bones with this paperweight.'

June Fordham's eyes widened and she swallowed convulsively.

'You can't frighten me like that, you know. I'll tell you, but you'll have to let me go first.'

With her mouth set in a determined line, Miss Digby Scott ripped off one of the strips of tape she had previously attached to the edge of the desk and placed it firmly over the bound woman's mouth.

'This is your last chance. Are you going to tell me?'

June Fordham shook her head violently and the Matron gave a deep sigh.

'Oh God, forgive me.' Her voice came out in an anguished whisper.

She lifted up the heavy paperweight

high in her right hand, closed her eyes and brought it down with every ounce of her strength. The glass landed on the bound woman's knuckles with a sickening thud and June Fordham's head jerked back, her whole body arching as if she had been electrocuted.

Diana Digby Scott was never to forget those next few minutes. She never knew how she managed to bring herself to hit the bound woman again, but she had to, twice more, before she was told about the concrete bunker behind the golf course.

Only when she had telephoned the resuscitation unit and the sergeant at the hotel did she lose control of herself. She staggered into the bathroom, was violently sick and then slumped on to her bed sobbing hysterically. She was weeping not only for what she had just done, but for the bitter misery of the last four years.

10

George Wainwright had had a frustrating afternoon. He had learned absolutely nothing, he was fed up to the back teeth with the sight of chemists' shops and photographic agents and to cap everything, his feet hurt.

He was having a pint in the bar when the receptionist brought Newton's note to him. He chuckled as he read it; now what was the Inspector doing with Nurse Carter on the golf course? Probably playing golf, he thought; Alison Carter did not sound the sort of girl for a bit on the side.

Wainwright felt a hint of disquiet when he saw the Rover in the hotel car park — surely Newton wouldn't have gone to the golf course without it. His uneasiness increased when he went outside and saw the ignition key in the switch. If there was one thing that Newton was careful about, it was locking up the car and with a thoughtful frown on his face, Wainwright got behind the wheel, or at least he tried to do so. The seat was so far forward on its runners, that he was unable to squeeze in without pushing it back. He and Newton were much the same height and as he drove towards the golf course, he was quite certain that something had gone badly wrong.

He went straight to the club-house and found the secretary in his office. The Colonel had met Newton on the previous day, but had neither seen nor heard of him that afternoon. He told Wainwright about the range behind the sixth hole and how to reach it by car and the sergeant drove out there, even walking up the length of the sandy track. He found nothing, no tracks, no foot-prints, no clue of any description.

He did not want to make a fool of himself by reporting Newton's disappearance too soon, particularly if he was up to something with Alison Carter, and went back to the hotel. After supper, he rang the hospital and after a long wait, got through to Sarah Bennett, who promised to see if she could find Alison. An hour later, she rang back to say that she had been missing all afternoon and that no one knew where she was.

Wainwright was on the point of phoning the Yard when the Matron's call came through. He was out of the hotel in a flash and as he turned into the main road, the tyres of the Rover screaming in protest, he glanced to his right and saw the ambulance, its blue light flashing, just pulling out of the hospital entrance. He went past it doing seventy and in no time, was braking for the turn into the road which ran by the side of the golf course. As he spun the wheel, he thought for a heart stopping moment that he had overdone it and that the Rover was going to turn over, but the front wheel, which had left the road, thumped down again and the powerful car went snaking up the narrow track.

He drove as far as he could, made sure that there was room for the ambulance to draw up alongside and pausing only long enough to snatch the torch from the glove pocket, sprinted for the concrete bunker.

There was only one that fitted the description and he wrenched at the rusty door handle. He almost fell as it turned with surprising ease, then the door burst open and the poisonous atmosphere hit him.

Wainwright switched on the torch and for a moment was stunned into inactivity by what he saw. Newton, his face and hair covered with sand, was sitting in his shirt sleeves with his back against some shelves, his head slumped forwards, while the girl, dressed only in the detective's jacket, was lying with her head in his lap.

For a moment, the sergeant thought they were both dead, but then he saw a faint movement from the girl's chest and he started to drag her outside. He had only just got her to the entrance when the team of doctors and nurses arrived and he stood aside to let the experts get on with it.

'Will they be all right?' he asked the doctor in charge ten minutes later.

'I think so; we made it just about in time. I'm not worried about the man, but I'm not so sure about the girl; she'll live, but whether or not she recovers completely depends on how long she was anoxic.' He saw Wainwright's puzzled expression. 'The brain can't do without oxygen for any length of time you know, and it was pretty foul in there.'

The girl still had a mask strapped to her face and as she was lifted into the ambulance, Newton was left unattended on a stretcher nearby. Wainwright knelt by his side anxiously and was relieved to see that the Inspector was already looking a better colour and was breathing quite easily.

'You're not such a bad bloke,' he said half aloud. 'I wonder if you made it with Nurse Carter.'

Wainwright's smile turned to an expression of horror as Newton opened one eye.

'I heard that George. You always were an insubordinate bastard.'

*　*　*

Six months later, Newton and Alison Carter were married in the country church in a village just outside Winchester. George Wainwright felt hopelessly out of place, the only man there, he was sure, who was not wearing a morning coat, and he tried to make himself as inconspicuous as possible at the reception. He felt a pang of jealousy when he saw Alison looking fresh and radiant in her beautiful wedding dress and even more, when he remembered only too vividly what she had looked like underneath.

He smiled when the couple approached him.

'Well, George?'

'Well, sir?' He saw that Alison had turned to speak to someone else and lowered his voice. 'I don't reckon I need to ask you a third time do I?'

The other man laughed and punched him playfully in the stomach. 'No, George, I don't think you need. You can take it that Nurse Carter and I are making out and for that matter, as you are wont to put it, very nicely indeed.'

'What was that you were saying Roger?'

'Nothing darling — just a private little joke between George here and me.'

'Nothing about the 'beast with two backs', I hope.'

George Wainwright watched them walk away, laughing uproariously at the expression on his face.

'You old bastard,' he said to himself, shaking his head in admiration and total disbelief. 'What have you done to her?'

REFLECTED GLORY

John Russell Fearn

When artist Clive Hexley, R. A. vanishes, Chief Inspector Calthorp of Scotland Yard is called upon to look into the disappearance, and his investigations lead him to question Hexley's ex-fiancée, Elsa Farraday. Elsa confesses that she has murdered the artist. The girl's peculiar manner puzzles Calthorp, and he hesitates to make an arrest, particularly as Hexley's body cannot be found. It is not until Calthorp calls in Dr. Adam Castle, the psychiatrist investigator, that the strange mystery of Elsa's behaviour and the artist's disappearance is solved.